— short, broad and strong as a bull, his heavy jowls vibrating as he thumped the top of the desk. 'How many times a day do we get inventors in this damned building, hey? Did you ever stop to add it up? All of them no good! In all London why do they have to pick on me? Kick him out — or at any rate tell the commissionaire to do it. I won't have anything to do with it!'

Janet Kayne sighed and picked up the card pensively.

'Then that's a pity, Mr. Drew. You know, it's his name that counts, far more than his invention — whatever it is. See what it says here? Rajek Quinton. That *means* something! He's a Swiss, and at one time he was the head of a famous firm of watchmakers.'

'Oh? How do you know that?'

'I saw an announcement about it when he came to England.'

Emerson Drew raised his eyebrows. 'So? Well, you're a better informed secretary than I realized, Miss Kayne. I still say I never heard of him and I don't suppose he's got anything any better than

1

'I never heard of him,' Emerson Drew said briefly, tossing the visiting card down on the shiny-topped desk. 'What does he want? Anyway, I thought I told you to keep strangers away from me, Miss Kayne? What's the good of me giving orders if you're going to do just as you like?'

'It's not exactly that, sir,' Janet Kayne interrupted, quite calmly. 'This is different. At least, I think it is . . . I believe you should see him.'

'Hmmm . . . ' Emerson Drew picked up the card again in a podgy, well scrubbed hand and meditated. Janet Kayne waited, noting how the fat rolled on her employer's neck as he moved his head. Then his sharp gray eyes fixed on her.

'*What's he got?*'

'Invention of some kind — '

'Invention!' Drew jumped to his feet

First published in Great Britain

First Linford Edition
published 2006

British Library CIP Data

Fearn, John Russell, *1908 – 1960*
    Account settled.—Large print ed.—
Linford mystery library
1. Detective and mystery stories
2. Large type books
I. Title
823.9′12 [F]

ISBN 1–84617–487–2

Published by
F. A. Thorpe (Publishing)
Anstey, Leicestershire

Set by Words & Graphics Ltd.
Anstey, Leicestershire
Printed and bound in Great Britain by
T. J. International Ltd., Padstow, Cornwall

This book is printed on acid-free paper

JOHN RUSSELL FEARN

ACCOUNT SETTLED

Complete and Unabridged

LINFORD
Leicester

ACCOUNT SETTLED

When scientist Rajek Quinton was pushed, screaming, down a mineshaft by Emerson Drew's hired killer, Drew and his co-conspirators Darnhome and de Brock were set to exploit Quinton's amazing invention. But he reckoned without Larry Clark of the C.I.D., and Quinton's genius. Larry, aided by Drew's secretary, Joyce Sutton, obtained the evidence needed to send Drew and his cohorts to their doom. But exactly who was Joyce Sutton? And did Quinton really die in the mud-filled pit shaft?

Other titles in the
Linford Mystery Library:

CRADLE SNATCH

Peter Conway

Mr. Justice Craythorne is convinced that Janice Beaton is a wicked woman and sentences her to three years in prison — but later he is to discover just how wicked she is. After kidnapping the judge's baby grandson, she proceeds to terrorise his family ... Cathy Weston leads the investigation but finds herself becoming emotionally involved with the baby's father. The physical and psychological pressures mount, and the young and vulnerable police inspector now finds herself targeted by Beaton and her sinister accomplice.

ODD WOMAN OUT

George Douglas

Chief Inspector Bill Hallam and sergeant 'Jack' Spratt of the Deniston C.I.D. are investigating the death of Madge Adkin. The dead woman had peculiar habits and claimed to be a bird-watcher, but knew nothing about birds. The trail they follow leads them to an escaped prisoner, an unorthodox 'healer' and a bunch of anonymous letters . . . The killer seems to have covered his tracks, but a blackmail attempt, quite unconnected with the murder, brings the detectives the proof they need.

the rest of these crazy inventors who think the Drew Combine is the gateway to El Dorado. But, anyway, show him in. Never know until you try.'

Janet Kayne nodded and went to the door. She was a thin, bony girl with high cheekbones and untroubled blue eyes. There were times when Emerson Drew wondered if anything would ever make her show emotion.

'Quinton,' he muttered, rubbing his flabby jaw. 'Of all the damned silly names!' He heaved back into his chair and sat down heavily to wait. It was not long before the door opened and Janet Kayne announced the visitor. Then she retired.

Drew sat with his brows down contemplating the man. He was middle-aged, short, well but quietly dressed, his white hair brushed back firmly from a broad forehead. In one hand he carried his soft black hat and in the other a briefcase.

'Mr. Quinton . . . ' Drew rose, hand extended. 'Glad to know you. Take a seat. Have a cigar?'

'Thank you, no. I'm a non-smoker.' Rajek Quinton had a well-modulated voice and spoke English perfectly. 'And I'm glad you could see me.'

'See you? But of course!' Drew beamed genially, selected a cigar for himself, lit it, and then returned to his chair. 'Nobody has any trouble seeing me! Now, sir, what's on your mind?'

'First, I think I had better make it clear to you that I am a Swiss.' Quinton laid the briefcase on the desk and Drew noted the remarkably slender hand. 'Until recently I carried on business as a watchmaker in my native country, and during this occupation I had the opportunity — the exact details of which I shall not divulge — to come into possession of certain plans. They were crude, undeveloped, at that time. I — er — made a point of developing them thoroughly.'

'So?' Drew was nodding sideways in his big chair, the cigar smoldering between his fingers.

'Despite my perfecting of the plans I found that in my own country there was

4

little use for them. I had reason to come to England, chiefly for the sake of my daughter who needs milder air than our home country. I've been in London now for about a month and I came to hear of you as a financier and interested in matters capable of — of, shall I say, producing a good monetary return?'

Drew puffed at his cigar for a while.

'Certainly this is the Drew Financial Trust,' he assented finally, 'and we are definitely interested in worthwhile inventions, finance, international barters, and so on. But it all depends on what you have to offer.'

'I have the Quinton self-sinking atomic bomb,' the Swiss said, without so much as a blink of his mild blue eyes.

'The . . . what?' Drew tried, with difficulty, to sound politely interested.

'In these days of science, Mr. Drew, any invention ahead of the general run — like electronics, rocket propulsion, atomic power, and so on, should be welcome.' Quinton unzipped his briefcase as he talked. 'I don't have to tell you that though the world is at peace there are deadly factions waiting for a convenient moment to start trouble again.'

'No,' Drew admitted heavily. 'You don't have to tell me.'

'Therefore we must be one jump ahead of everybody else, as our American friends would phrase it. I have asked the War Office here to interest themselves but there were such delays, so much difficulty in getting to the fountain head, I decided to see if I could get some action out of you. Here, sir, is the plan — or rather the blueprint.'

Drew took it and flattened its curling ends with the palms of his hands. Wheezing, he spread it out on the desk and gazed at it. Quinton got to his feet and came over to him, began tracing out important details with a long, immaculate finger.

'You may or may not be scientist enough to grasp the idea, sir,' he said presently. 'Stated briefly, it is this: An atom, as all scientists agree and as many laymen know, is analogous — at least in the matter of scale — to a kind of miniature solar system, a nucleus like a sun, with a greater or lesser number of electrons moving round it like planets. You understand?'

'Go on, anyway,' Drew suggested.

'In ordinary iron, for instance, the molecules have north and south poles like all other molecules, but they point in every possible direction, indiscriminately. The molecules have magnetism in them but it isn't organized. Pointing haphazardly though each is a small magnet, they tend in the mass to cancel each other out. It is when the whole mass is magnetized that all the poles point in one particular direction . . . '

Drew shifted uncomfortably and considered the end of his cigar.

'This explanation, sir, is essential,' Quinton said, noting the ill-concealed irritability. 'Not only atoms possess poles but molecules as well — and they are just as indiscriminate. But, if all the poles point in *one* direction only it means that they become parallel, blocking so small a portion of the space they normally occupy that they can pass right through ordinary matter. Matter becomes penetrable and, to the bomb, has about the same resistance as very thick oil. If the bomb is placed on the floor, say, with its magnetic apparatus working, it will sink into that floor, drawn by the force of gravity. Wherever it may settle — and it vanishes from sight immediately it sinks below surface — it remains as a deadly hidden danger until the time-fuse fires it. You must see the advantages! The bombs can go anywhere, through anything, and remain hidden!'

Drew sat back in his chair again and considered.

'Have you a working model, Mr. Quinton?'

'Er — yes, but — well, naturally, I don't want to put all my cards on the table at once.'

'Quite! Wise man!' Drew nodded vigorously. 'I'll tell you frankly, you seem to have an idea here which is years ahead of present scientific progress, as far as military armament is concerned anyway.'

'You can be sure of one thing, Mr. Drew, and that is that I have spoken the truth. I have been a master-watchmaker since the age of twenty, and the making of this intricate bomb with its small magnet controls and scientific devices is one of the finest things I ever did. Of course it took me a long time to work out the model. Now it has been done the duplicating will be easy. I'm quite certain it will do all that I claim for it.'

'I'm not doubting it — but I don't pretend to be a scientist. I am the financial head of this organization, not the man with the brains . . . ' Drew grinned widely and showed his strong white teeth for a moment. 'I'm interested — definitely interested, but you'll have to leave this plan with me for study by my experts before I can go any further. If they are satisfied, that's good enough for me. We'll soon come to terms.'

Quinton returned to his chair thoughtfully and seemed to reflect for a moment or two.

'Your experts can, of course, arrive at only one conclusion,' he said finally. 'And that being so you might as well know my terms now. I shall want a million pounds in advance royalties, and the balance of terms to be arranged.'

Some of the cordiality left Drew's face and it became much more like that of a bulldog.

'A million pounds! After all, Mr. Quinton, that's a colossal sum!'

'It's a colossal invention, and it's not a big sum compared to the international value — and danger — of the thing! It might even be worth a million to keep me quiet!' Quinton shrugged. 'However, I merely tell you my figure beforehand so that you will know how to plan accordingly. I certainly will not take less. As for the blueprint . . . '

He stopped, frowning hard.

'You shall have an undertaking and receipt for it,' Drew said. 'I can understand your reluctance, but if you won't leave it we can't do business — and there it is. After all, the Drew Financial Trust is not a firm that is here today and gone tomorrow, you know.'

'True, but — . You couldn't have your scientists examine it here and now, while I wait?'

Drew shook his head. His gray hair was

cropped so closely it resembled plush.

'Afraid not. It's the work of many hours to be sure of every detail. We may even have to make a working model before we can be certain.'

Quinton still meditated, then at last he nodded.

'Very well, then. Let me have your receipt.'

Drew pressed a button on his desk and Janet Kayne entered silently. Drew looked across at her.

'Oh, Miss Kayne, make out an undertaking for Mr. Quinton — In consideration of him allowing us to have — er — Blueprint Number 7670/K, we undertake — . And so on. You know. Right away please.'

'Very good, Mr. Drew.'

The door closed again and Quinton aimed questioning blue eyes.

'How long do you think it will be before you know something definite?'

Drew reflected briefly. 'It's important enough to get on with right away. We ought to know something by this time tomorrow at the latest.'

Rajek Quinton nodded quietly and for a moment or two Drew studied him.

'Business apart, Mr. Quinton,' he said at length, 'how do you like being in England?'

A faint smile crossed the inventor's lean, pale features.

'I don't, really — but as I told you my daughter's health comes first. Unfortunately she has heart disease, and it's a very big worry for me.'

'Hmm. I'm sorry to hear that. Is she — young?'

'Twenty-five — and most capable. You see — ' Quinton moved as though his words had suddenly become distasteful to him — 'I'm staking pretty well everything on this invention, Mr. Drew. I sold out my watchmaker business, but it didn't realize a very great deal, certainly not enough money to live in the style my daughter and I would like. I want, if I can, to get into a high social niche in this country, and my daughter too, of course. We undoubtedly will if you and I come to terms. At the moment you can reach me at the Grand Hotel in Fennis Street.'

Drew jotted down the address on his scratchpad. He was looking quite amiable again now.

'And if we come to terms do you propose to stay in London?'

'I think not. We prefer the country. We have ideas about a quiet place up in the north east.'

'And yet I believe you mentioned milder air?

'The north east of England is far milder than Switzerland, Mr. Drew, and there's a lot of quiet countryside up there.'

'Mmm, true — '

Drew broke off as Janet Kayne returned, a quarto sheet embossed with the Trust seals in her hand. Drew took it, added his signature, then handed it across to Quinton. 'There you are, sir — everything in order.'

Quinton looked at it and put it in his briefcase. The only sound for a moment was of the zipper closing, then the inventor got to his feet.

'I'll be here this time tomorrow, Mr. Drew,' he said. 'And thank you.'

The financier rose and shook hands, went with Quinton as far as the office door, then, when he had shown him out, he stood for a moment and pondered, his hand on the knob. Janet Kayne straightened up from the desk, glanced briefly at the blueprint and set it on one side.

'Miss Kayne — '

'Sir?' She glanced up expectantly as Drew came over to her ponderously.

'Have Mr. Valant come in here from the research department right away, will you?'

The girl nodded and went out. Still pensive, pulling at his cigar, Drew unrolled the blueprint again and contemplated it. He was still doing so when Bruce Valant, the lanky chief of the scientific research department, came in. He had light-colored eyes and his wiry hair bushed up around his head.

'Want me, Mr. Drew?'

'Yes. Take a look at this and tell me how good or bad it is. A good deal depends on it.'

The scientist flattened the blueprint out and brooded over it. Drew stood watching, the fragrance from his cigar drifting into his eyes.

'Off hand,' Valant said at length, straightening up, 'I'd say this is some newfangled sort of bomb. From the look of this blueprint — crazy though it sounds — it looks as though the bomb would pass through the interstices of matter to any desired depth, drawn by the pull of earth's own gravity.'

Drew nodded his shaven head approvingly.

'Good! I can see I don't pay for nothing in having you, Valant. That's exactly what the thing is. I want you to rush through a model of it and see just how efficient it is — say, by eight o'clock tonight.'

The scientist shook his wild-haired head dubiously.

'That won't be too easy, sir. There's some pretty intricate workmanship here — '

'Quinton told me that a copy model from these designs would not take long, and I want it done!' Drew set his jaw. 'Drop everything else, commandeer all the labor and money you need, but get this model ready for eight tonight.'

Valant rolled the print up and nodded. He knew it was impossible to argue with Emerson Drew when he got hold of a pet idea.

'I'll do it, sir,' he promised, and headed for the door.

'And another thing, Valant — '

'Yes, sir?'

'Don't let anybody else see the print. Put your workers on separate sections and never let the entire set-up get out of your hands. I'm holding you responsible.'

The scientist nodded and went out. Drew sat down at the desk again and pulled a telephone to him, dialed on the private wire.

'That you, J.K.?' he asked presently.

The heavy, chesty voice of Joseph K. Darnhome, head of the Darnhome Metals Corporation, answered.

'Who'd you think it was, man? Couldn't be anybody else on this line, could it?'

'All right, all right, don't get touchy — or is it your liver again? Anyway, I rang to tell you that I think we're on to something, and if I'm any judge it's worth a fortune several times over.'

'Well, your judgment has been pretty accurate all the time I've known you so I don't see any reason why it should fail now. What is it?'

'I don't even trust the private wire to tell you that. Enough for me to say that it's worth your while to be over here in my office this evening at eight sharp. You'll get the surprise of your life!'

'Well, I — ' J.K. hesitated, then he seemed to make up his mind. 'All right, Drew, I'll be there. I'm afraid the wife will play hell. I was going to take her out.'

'Eight it is,' Drew said briefly, and put the phone back on its cradle. He waited a second or two and then dialed another number. This time the high, acrimonious voice of Marvin de Brock floated to him. De Brock, head of Independent Atomics, had no time for anybody outside of himself. He was only civil with Emerson Drew because he had to be. Drew was the mastermind — finance.

'Eight o'clock, eh?' de Brock repeated querulously, when Drew had uttered practically the same words as to Darnhome.

17

'You choose a damned awkward time, don't you?'

'If you can't take time out to put yourself in line with more money you're more self-centered than I thought,' Drew snapped. 'Of course I can always get — '

'No, no,' de Brock interrupted. 'I'll be there.'

'Good!'

Drew put the telephone down and rubbed his hands gently together.

2

Jaline Quinton was waiting for her father when he came into the entrance lounge of the Grand Hotel. She saw him enter through the revolving doors, got to her feet hurriedly and went across to him.

'Well, dad, how did it go?' She spoke in her native tongue.

'Oh, hello, Jal . . . ' Her father smiled at her, did not resist as she led him across to the wicker chairs under the dried palms where she had been seated. 'I didn't think you'd be back so soon.'

'Nothing else for it,' the girl answered, sighing. 'The post was filled. Don't seem to be many people who want an interpreter these days. You'd think that with a knowledge of seven languages I'd get a good deal further than this.'

Her serious blue eyes regarded him for a moment. She was a good-looking girl of obviously Teutonic descent. Blonde hair was piled in coils and waves on top of her head and about her ears. She was slender-shouldered, elfin-limbed, with features which had the pink and white delicacy begotten of her cardiac trouble.

'And you?' she asked. 'How did you get on?'

'I think Mr. Drew will be able to do something for me — '

'Then — then you don't *know*? You showed him the blueprint, didn't you?'

'Of course — but I had to leave it with him for examination. His research department has to go through it.'

Jaline considered him in troubled silence for a moment.

'I know what you're thinking,' he said, setting the briefcase down on the chair beside him. 'That I shouldn't have done that. I had to, Jal; there was no other way. No scientist could decide the value of my invention by a mere glance. I'm going back tomorrow morning for the answer. I have a receipt so there's nothing whatever to worry about.''

'If ever there was a man with no business acumen and a frightening trust of his fellow men, it's you, dad,' the girl sighed. 'You built that watch-making firm of yours up into a concern worth a fortune, and then you let it go for a paltry fifty thousand pounds, English value. Now you have an invention that is again worth millions and you actually leave the blueprint in the hands of a man about whom you know nothing, trusting solely to a receipt. Do you realize what you've done?'

Quinton smiled and patted the girl's hand. 'I have copies of the print, my dear. Everything will be all right, don't you worry. Drew is too well-known as a financier to try any shady tricks. Wouldn't pay him.'

'I wonder . . . ' Jaline reflected. 'I don't trust financiers — not the big ones anyway — no more than you trust banks. Remember how you had your cheque for fifty thousand changed into notes when you got to England and now have it stored away in your trunk upstairs? Well, you're afraid of banks, just as I am of financiers . . . Y'know, dad, what I really wish is — ' The girl's voice trailed off and she shrugged. 'What's the use of my talking?'

'What? What do you really wish?'

'That we could go back to Switzerland, retire on the fifty thousand, and forget everything. England and London are not the places for us, dad. I'm unhappy. That's why I'm trying to liven things up by looking for a post of some kind.'

Her father looked at her steadily. 'We can't go back to our own country, Jal — and you know it. We've got to remember what the specialists said.'

'About my heart, you mean? That only softer air could prolong my life? That's all medical talk and I don't believe one half of it. Let's go back, the moment we have Drew's answer!'

Quinton shook his head slowly.

'No, my dear, I wouldn't take the risk; not with your heart in its present state. If we went back and the air braced you so much as to — to kill you, just think how I'd feel!'

Jaline shrugged. 'All right, then, we'll just have to carry on in London — or out in the north-east country somewhere. Perhaps we'd better discuss it tomorrow when we've heard what Drew has to say.'

'That,' her father agreed quietly, 'would probably be the best.'

*   *   *

At eight o'clock that evening the shades were tightly drawn over the windows in Emerson Drew's immense office and the concealed lighting glowed on the furniture and roughcast walls in shadowless brilliance.

He sat at the desk, square and complacent, contemplating the finished model of the Quinton bomb. On his right was the pale-faced, lean-cheeked Metals tycoon — J.K. Darnhome, his cold gray eyes studying the bomb's smooth, tapering outlines.

Marvin de Brock, acid-faced, black-haired, fiftyish, had his elbows on the desk and his chin cradled in his hands. His expression was one of profound absorption.

'And you are sure,' Drew asked Bruce Valant, the scientist, slowly, 'that everything is perfect? That Quinton really knows what he is up to?'

'Beyond a doubt,' the scientist agreed, standing on the opposite side of the desk. 'Suppose I demonstrate the thing for you then you'll get the right idea . . . '

Drew nodded, waved a hand and sat back in his chair. Valant picked up the bomb and took it across to a sheet of two-inch-thick steel that he had brought in. The steel formed the top of a table, collapsible legs supporting it on each side.

'Observe, gentlemen,' Valant said, after setting the bomb's internal mechanism in operation.

He put the bomb nose-down on the steel plate and before the eyes of the astonished men the object began to sink gently through the tabletop until its entire length had made the transition and it dropped like a gigantic metallic pear to the carpet.

Immediately Valant whipped it up and stopped the mechanism.

'It looks,' Marvin de Brock said, musing, 'just like a conjuring trick. One of those matter-through-matter illusions.'

'With one difference, gentlemen, that this is *not* an illusion,' Valant said. He unfastened the steel plate from the legs and stood it endwise on the desk. There was not a trace of rupture or marking where the bomb had been.

'Miraculous!' J.K. Darnhome breathed, pushing a lock of fallen gray hair out of his eye.

'Simply the utilization of scientific facts,' Valant said, shrugging. 'Quinton has found a way to make matter pass through matter by forcing the atoms to obey magnetism, and thereby their normal obstructive power is neutralized. It's brilliant — no doubt of it.''

Drew nodded slowly and motioned the scientist to put the bomb on the desk.

'That's all for now, Valant. You can go home if you want. Thanks for getting the job done.'

The scientist nodded and left the room. Drew gave a slow, grim smile and then glanced at the men to either side of him.

'Well, gentlemen, was it worth your while getting here for eight o'clock, or not?'

'Oh, it was worth it,' J.K. agreed. 'Just as you said, the thing is worth a fortune . . . How much does this chap Quinton want for it?'

Drew reached out for a cigar box and held it forth.

'A million advance in respect of royalties, and the remaining terms to be arranged.'

'Then he's crazy,' Marvin de Brock commented, striking his lighter. 'Give him a thousand and he'll think himself lucky.'

'I do not propose,' Drew said, closing the box emphatically, to give him *anything*! I've seen him; you have not, and believe me I doubt if a more simple-minded soul ever descended from heaven straight into the lion's den.'

'Many inventors are apparently quiet,' Darnhome reflected. 'But when you start to cross them they blow up in your face. I don't trust the quiet type. Never did.'

'I don't think Rajek Quinton falls into the category you're thinking of, J.K.,' Drew said, shaking his head. 'In fact, the thing is so easy it's nearly a shame to do it. Here, right in our grasp, is the blueprint for an invention worth millions. I could, of course, photocopy it, manufacture secretly, and have the original blueprint returned to Quinton with the simple statement that his invention doesn't interest us. But that wouldn't do us any good. He'd submit it elsewhere and we'd perhaps find ourselves saddled with stiff opposition before very long. So, I see only one way out . . . '

The huge office was quiet for a moment. Marvin de Brock found himself staring at the sinister outlines of the thing that held unlimited power.

'You mean — dispose of him?' Darnhome's voice was sober.

'There have been times,' Drew answered, 'when disposal of a certain irritating faction has been necessary, just in the course of business. I don't hide the fact from either of you because you yourselves were in at those disposals. Remember Travers of New York? Then there was the case of L'Estrage of Paris, a necessary extermination. I'm afraid we have similar necessary extermination here.'

De Brock rubbed his chin and scowled.

Darnhome looked across at the cocktail cabinet and decided he needed a drink.

'This is no time for your damned whisky, J.K.!' Drew snapped, turning.

'Any time's the time for that . . .' The tycoon went over to the cabinet, poured out three glasses of whisky and brought them across to the desk.

'Are you sure that nothing can backfire if we dispose of Quinton?' de Brock asked.

'I'm absolutely sure. I got quite a bit of information out of him without him knowing why I was fishing. He's only been in England a month, and he can't have made many friends in that time. He's here because of his daughter's health — heart disease or something. Anyway, she needs softer air.'

Darnhome drained his whisky glass and reflected.

'Sounds easy enough, if neatly done. Stranger in town with an invalid daughter.'

'Hardly an invalid,' de Brock corrected. 'Even if you have got heart disease you can sometimes skip around and fool everybody. I don't like the daughter angle, myself. Girls get outraged ideas sometimes when their fathers mysteriously vanish. How old is she?'

'Twenty-five.'

'I dislike it still more,' de Brock said, and picked up his glass.

'Well, a venture with no element of risk simply doesn't exist,' Drew said, shrugging. 'The fact remains that you, de Brock, represent Atomic Power; that you, J.K., control Metals, and that I have control of science and finance. Combined, we comprise a triumvirate of infinite power, and into our hands has come the wherewithal to add to our millions — not by manufacturing this bomb for our own country, but for *other* countries, who, as we know, are just waiting for an invention like this in order to retrieve their shattered fortunes. Atomic explosive in an unlimited number of Quinton bombs can bring any country to its knees in twenty-four hours. I do not propose to let the inventor of such an idea *live*. It would be suicidal.'

'All right,' de Brock said, after consideration. 'I'm with you. What about you, J.K.?'

Darnhome shrugged. 'As far as I'm concerned an inventor is neither here nor there where business is concerned . . . What do you propose doing, Drew?'

'You can leave that to me. I haven't failed before on a job of this kind, and I shan't this time. There's a little matter of a receipt that I shall have to attend to. Quinton has that. You need have no fear but what it will be recovered. One thing, though, we must all understand!' Drew looked at both impressively in turn. 'The actual secret of the Quinton bomb is ours alone — and that of Valant, my chief scientist. It must go no further than that. I will attend to the scientific end and the financing thereof; you, de Brock, will supply the atomic explosive from your organization — and you, J.K., the necessary metals. I'll make the necessary international contacts. That agreed?'

The other two men nodded slowly. Drew sat back and rubbed his hands.

'Good! With Quinton eliminated, and his daughter taken care of if she shows any signs of getting inquisitive, we've nothing to stop us cleaning up the biggest thing yet. Just let me handle it, gentlemen, and I'll let you know how things work out.'

They got to their feet and went over to the stand for their coats. In another few minutes they left, Drew thoughtfully contemplating the bomb upon his desk. He sat nearly motionless for three minutes, pulling at his cigar — and then at last he raised the telephone.

'Get me a Mr. Quinton at the Grand Hotel,' he told the night switch-girl.

'Yes, Mr. Drew.'

After a moment or two of cross-talking the inventor's voice came over the wire.

'Ah, Mr. Quinton.' Drew oozed magnanimity. 'I've been going into the matter of your — er — blueprint, but it's going to take longer than I anticipated. Maybe a week. Besides, there are one or two other details I'd like to discuss with you.'

'Of course. I'll come over and have a chat right away if you like — '

'No, no that won't be necessary. Tomorrow morning will do nicely, as we arranged — but I want you to bring that receipt with you and I'll give you another one, extending the time we are allowed to keep the blueprint. Understand?'

'Er — yes,' Quinton replied, though he sounded vague.

'Also,' Drew went on, 'I'd be glad of your model and what ever notes and other blueprints you may have in connection with this invention. They can all be included on the new receipt if you'd care to bring them.'

'Willingly, Mr. Drew. I'm only too glad to co-operate. Tell me, do you think I have something that really interests you?'

'There's no doubt of that,' Drew answered calmly. 'I think we'll be able to come to terms. Now look here, I don't like the thought of a valuable man like you bringing such plans through London either on foot or in a taxi. I'll send my private car for you. It'll be there at ten-thirty tomorrow morning. Just so as you can be sure, my chauffeur's name is Brant.'

'That's very good of you, Mr. Drew — '

'Not a bit. I'll see you tomorrow then. Goodbye.'

' 'Bye . . . '

Drew put the phone back on its cradle and then pressed a switch on the interphone box. A gruff voice answered.

'Yes, Mr. Drew?

'Brant? Come up to my office a moment.'

'Yessir.'

Drew waited until his chauffeur came from the staff room at the base of the great building. It took him five minutes, then he came striding into the room in his purple livery, peaked cap in hand. He was an iron-necked, square-jawed man of medium height, and being a chauffeur was not his only vocation. In fact only the power of Drew kept Douglas Brant out of the reach of the law.

'I've a job for you, Brant — ' Drew looked at him across the desk. 'Tomorrow morning at ten-thirty sharp you will arrive in the car at the Grand Hotel in Fennis Street and pick up a Swiss by the name of Rajek Quinton. You may even be asked if his daughter can come, too. If so, don't raise any objections. You will bring them straight here. You will ask Quinton if he has got everything: say *I* told you to ask that. Clear so far?'

The bullet head nodded.

'You will drive Quinton here. When he leaves here you will head in the direction of the Grand Hotel, but he must never get there. He must be — lost, and you get from him a receipt that he will be carrying with him. It will have my name on it.'

'Yes, sir,' the chauffeur agreed briefly. 'As in the ease of that French bloke L'Estrage and that other fellow Travers, from New York, you mean?'

'Exactly. And make a good job of it. No chance of recognition afterwards.'

'And supposing the daughter is there, too? What do I do then?'

Drew spread his podgy hands and smiled. 'Like father, like daughter. You need not discriminate.'

'I'll see to it, sir. Anything more?

'Not in that direction.' Drew got to his feet. 'I'm leaving now. You can drive me home.'

3

At 10-25 the following morning Rajek Quinton was in the lounge of the Grand Hotel, pacing slowly up and down, hat and topcoat on, his briefcase in one hand and a small cardboard box containing his model bomb in the other. Seated at one of the wicker tables watching him was Jaline.

'I don't often see you so excited, dad,' she remarked, smiling.

'Who wouldn't be?' He came over to her. 'This may mean a real fortune . . . the acknowledgment of my genius as a watchmaker, apart from the million advance and royalties to follow. With all that money we'll really be able to do as we want.'

'For that matter we could do on the fifty thousand.'

'Only within limits, my dear — to live as we want to live. I need a lot of money as working capital for other inventions and materials. Fifty thousand doesn't go far when costly materials are needed.'

'Well . . . ' A tiny frown marred the girl's forehead. 'I only hope things work out right. Silly of me to be so doubting, I suppose, but somehow — '

'Silly? Of course it is!' Quinton patted her shoulder. 'Drew has made it perfectly obvious that he's playing straight by asking me to come over again this morning, and even sending his car for me to go in — Ah!' Quinton glanced up as a stocky, bull-necked chauffeur in purple livery came through the revolving doors. 'This is probably the chap now . . . '

He raised his hand in a signal and Brant nodded and came over, touching his peaked cap.

''Morning, sir. Mr. Quinton?'

'That's right. You're Brant, Mr. Drew's chauffeur?'

'Yes, sir. The car's waiting outside. Mr. Drew asked me to remind you to bring everything.'

Quinton nodded and smiled. 'That's all right. Everything is here. Well, Jal, I'll be back soon . . . 'Bye for now.'

She nodded a farewell and Brant followed the inventor's short, well-dressed figure across the lounge and out through the revolving doors. In ten minutes they had reached the Drew Building and for the time being Brant's task was over. Quinton stepped into the elevator and was whisked to the seventh floor.

He found Emerson Drew awaiting him, smiling, advancing across the office with extended hand.

'Glad you could make it, Mr. Quinton. Have a seat and a cig — Or did you say you don't smoke?'

'That's right,' Quinton acknowledged, smiling. 'I don't.'

He put his case and box on the desk and settled his hat in his lap as he sat down.

'Well, sir, we've made progress ... ' Drew returned to his chair on the opposite side or the desk and nodded his plush-covered head. 'And there's no doubt that we'll take up the option on your invention *and* on the terms you suggested.'

'You mean — the million advance?'

Quinton asked slowly, his blue eyes fixed on the square face.

'I do. But of course that can't come immediately. There are the final tests to make, with actual explosive and so forth. I asked you to come so as to be certain that we have all the necessary formulae and, as it were, the spare parts in connection with the invention. We cannot go any further without being certain that the rights are exclusively ours. In a matter as vital as this, competition could be very dangerous. Understand?'

'Of course,' Quinton agreed, unzipping the briefcase and drawing out a blueprint and several papers. 'Here is the duplicate blueprint I retained for my own use. It is identical with the one you have and there are no other copies. And here is the mathematical formula and notes, together with my own private observations. Nothing else remains that has any connection with the bomb.'

'Splendid!' Drew exclaimed, studying the notes and blueprint in turn. 'All right, Mr. Quinton, this is all we need. I'll take your old receipt and give you a fresh one.'

Quinton nodded and handed it across. Drew's hand reached out to the bell-push and presently Janet Kayne entered, as severely dressed and imperturbable as usual.

'Yes. Mr. Drew?'

'Miss Kayne, draw up an undertaking for Mr. Quinton and in it state cancellation of this receipt I have here and instead give our undertaking to take full possession of all details, prints, and formulae on the Quinton bomb, in consideration of the advance royalty sum of one million pounds sterling, to be paid immediately upon completion of tests. That's the gist of it. You know how to put it. Do it right away and I'll sign it.'

'Yes, sir.'

Janet Kayne went out leaving the two men talking of irrelevancies. She returned with the completed document in ten minutes and laid it on the blotter.

'Good,' Drew acknowledged. 'I'll need you shortly to take some letters.'

'Yes, sir.'

Drew signed the document and with a smile gave it into Quinton's outstretched hand. The inventor smiled faintly, folded the sheet up and put it in his wallet.

'This has done me more good than you realize, Mr. Drew,' he said seriously. 'Though I never doubted but what you'd see the worth of the invention once you'd tried it.'

'We definitely do,' Drew assented, getting to his feet. 'You just leave everything to me and I'll give you a ring the moment matters are complete. Say in about three days. How's that?'

'I'll be waiting for it.' Quinton rose and took up his hat and briefcase. 'And thanks again.'

'As to that — ' Drew opened the door for him. 'I should be thanking you for your genius. Men as brilliant as you, Mr. Quinton are all too rare — Oh, the car will be waiting outside. Brant will take you wherever you wish to go.'

Quinton nodded, shook hands, and went off down the corridor. Drew stood looking after him, a grim smile on his heavy mouth; then he turned back into his office, perched himself on the edge of the desk facing the window and dialed on the private wire.

Silently Janet Kayne entered through the interconnecting doorway, regarded her employer's broad back, and hesitated.

'Hello, J.K.?' Drew's voice was full of easy cordiality. 'It's all fixed up. Thought I'd better tell you. Come over to my place tonight and we'll arrange the final details. Yes, right! Goodbye.'

Janet Kayne waited, contemplating her notebook. Drew put the telephone down for a second or two, dialed another number, then picked the instrument up again.

'De Brock? Everything's okay. Come over to my place tonight and we'll have a pow-wow. I've asked J.K. to come along. What? Sure! Couldn't have been easier. We've got the whole works. Nothing to worry about. Yes, see you tonight.'

The telephone rattled in its cradle and Drew slid off the desk, smiling. He gave a start as he saw Janet Kayne.

'What the devil are you doing here?' he demanded, glaring.

'You mentioned some letters for me to take down, sir — '

'Is that any reason why you have to

creep in when my back's turned? Why didn't you knock?'

'I did, sir — lightly. Perhaps you didn't hear.'

Drew hesitated, compressed his lips, then sat down. He motioned the girl to a chair. She began taking the letters as he snapped them out. Half an hour later she departed into her own office again. By ten to twelve she had finished the letters and took them in for Drew's signature.

'I'll sign them later,' he said briefly. 'Go to your lunch and come back ten minutes earlier. Suit me better that way. I've no appointments for this afternoon, have I?'

'No, sir. A clean sheet.'

'Right. That's all.'

Janet Kayne nodded and left the office, returned to her own quarters to don hat and coat. As poker-faced as ever she went to the elevator and so down to the ground floor. She was crossing the wide pseudo-marble entrance ball when a slender, blonde-headed girl came in at the swing doors with anxious movements. She took three strides across the shining floor and then paused, putting a hand to her forehead and swaying noticeably.

'Here, what's the matter?' Janet Kayne put an arm about the girl's shoulder and supported her tightly. From the distance the commissionaire began to appear.

'I'm — I'm sorry,' the girl apologized, trying to smile. 'I just feel a — a little faint . . . '

'This way,' Janet Kayne said, completely in control of the situation, and waving the commissionaire away she helped the girl across to one of the long oak forms and settled her down.

Very gradually, as she sat relaxed with head thrown back, color began to return to the girl's cheeks. She made a little gesture.

'You're very kind to bother over me like this — '

'I hope I'm human,' Janet Kayne responded. 'You feeling better now?'

'Yes. Yes, indeed. Much better. It's my heart that's the trouble, I'm afraid, and anxiety doesn't improve it. Tell me, do you work in this building? I'm Jaline Quinton.'

'Oh! Your father was here this morning — '

'Then he did *get* here all right?'

'Why, certainly!' Janet Kayne's eyebrows rose ever so slightly. 'Any reason why he shouldn't? Incidentally, I'd better explain. I am Janet Kayne, personal secretary to Mr. Drew.'

'Then I couldn't have met a better person!' Jaline Quinton seemed by now to have completely recovered. 'I'm wondering what has happened to my father. Have you any idea what time he left here?'

'I should think it would be about quarter to eleven.'

'Then — ' Worry came back to Jaline Quinton's face. 'Then where *is* he? He said he'd come straight back to the hotel. Even if he walked it he could do it within half an hour — and now it's noon! I'm terribly worried. That's why I came along to see if I could find him.'

Jaline's eyes met the secretary's level, impersonal ones for a moment. Janet Kayne raised and lowered her shoulders gently.

'I'm sure there must be quite a reasonable explanation, Miss Quinton.

44

After all, not very much time has gone by. Your father may have called somewhere and — '

'But you don't understand! My father came here about his invention and every moment he's out of my sight I'm scared for his safety.'

'Then I'm sure you needn't be. He arrived here safely with all the details of his invention. I know, because I typed out the receipt. If you take my advice, Miss Quinton, you'll go back to the hotel where I'm sure you'll find your father waiting for you. By this time *he* is probably the anxious one.'

Jaline got to her feet and nodded worriedly — then both she and Janet Kayne glanced towards the elevator as the gates clanged back. Emerson Drew himself emerged in topcoat and black soft hat, gold-knobbed cane in his hand.

He glanced briefly towards the two women, let his eyes rest for a moment on his secretary, then following his usual custom outside the office he took no further notice and proceeded on his way to the outdoors.

'That's Mr. Drew,' Janet Kayne explained quietly. 'And I'm afraid I must be moving on. Perhaps I could see you as far as the end of the street?'

'No, thanks all the same.' Jaline Quinton squared her shoulders. 'I'll be all right — really. I soon get over these bad spells of mine.'

Nevertheless, Janet Kayne took the girl's arm firmly as they walked side by side towards the swing doors.

★   ★   ★

At the very moment the two women were leaving the Drew Building Rajek Quinton was recovering from the stupefying effects of an ether-soaked handkerchief. As consciousness drifted back to him in snatches he remembered bits and pieces — vaguely, clouded by the miasma of dreams.

He had got into the car. Brant had driven in quite normal fashion amidst the traffic, then complaining of engine trouble he had turned down a side street and stopped . . . Then what? Dully,

46

Quinton remembered. He had said he would get out and walk — but he had been forced back into the car with that handkerchief over his face, had collapsed in a corner seat as though asleep. And now —

He opened his eyes and for a moment or two his brain swam. Then he became aware that he was out in the country somewhere. There was a dry rustling of grass, a warm breeze fanning his face. Above him was pale autumn sky and the sound of an active bird.

Gradually Quinton propped himself on his elbow and found he was lying in the grass beside a hedge. Not far away, leaning on the wire beside the hedge, was Brant, smoking a cigarette.

'Better, Mr. Quinton?' he asked briefly, and threw the cigarette down to grind it under his heel.

'Better — ?' Quinton staggered up and stood staring at the stocky, powerful chauffeur fixedly. 'What the devil are you talking about? You made me unconscious with that ether!'

'That's right,' Brant agreed, straightening.

'Just so's to keep you quiet while I got you out here. We're about twenty miles from anywhere — and you're not going back!'

'I'm not — ' Quinton's head swam again. 'W-what did you say?'

'You've come to the end of the road!' Brant regarded him with small, merciless eyes. 'I've got a job to do — and I'll do it proper, as I always do. See those wooden props standing up over there?' He pointed behind him.

Quinton looked wonderingly and nodded.

'They're disused copper mines,' Brant explained. 'And there's no better place for getting rid o' folks. Quagmire at the bottom and it takes care of everything. But just in case it doesn't — in case your body isn't sucked down as it should be, there's a second precaution for making you unrecognizable.'

Quinton drew a deep breath and clenched his fists.

'What the devil are you talking about?' he demanded fiercely. 'You lay a hand on me and I'll — '

'No, you won't,' Brant interrupted. 'I've got it all planned, and I've got your wallet, including the receipt Mr. Drew gave you. Vital for me to have that. There's no identification beyond the clothes you stand up in. And your face — and neither of 'em will count for much in a moment, either!'

Before Quinton could understand what was intended, Brant stooped and picked up a flat metal bowl that had been lying in the grass. Very carefully he balanced it on his palm. There appeared to be water in it and Quinton watched curiously.

'I filled this while you were unconscious,' Brant explained. 'Same as I took your wallet. *Here it comes*!'

Quinton half turned, as though to run — then the water-like liquid in the bowl landed in his face and across his suit. Instantly he screamed at the frightful anguish of pure nitric acid as it ate deep into his flesh. Blindly, words came tumbling out of his mouth, he fell on his knees and clawed at his face. The acid trickled corrosively through his clutching fingers.

'Only sure way to destroy identity,' Brant told him. 'Now come on — '

He grabbed him by the arm and forced him, screaming hoarsely, across the rough grass towards the mine planks. Then he gave him a mighty shove. Blindly, sobbing now with the pain of the acid, Quinton heaved over the edge of the mineshaft and pitched downwards.

Brant stood waiting, listening, his square jaw set tightly. At last he heard it — the deep, soggy thud of the body striking the quagmire at the bottom of the shaft. A low sigh escaped him and he lit another cigarette. He delayed several minutes more and then at last he turned and walked back to where he left the emptied bowl of acid. He picked it up carefully and returned it to the car in the roadway. Silently he drove away down the deserted country lane.

It was half-past two when he entered Emerson Drew's office and found the big man alone, browsing through the papers on the desk. Drew said nothing, but his hard gray eyes had an unmistakable question in them.

Brant nodded slowly in confirmation and placed the wallet on the desk, then he stood and watched in silence, as Drew went through it.

'And there is no chance of him returning?' Drew asked, when his examination was finished.

'None,' Brant replied with conviction. 'Nor is there any chance of identification if the body should ever be found. I can give you the details, sir — if you want them.'

Drew shook his shaven head. 'No. I'll take your word for it. That's all for now, Brant.'

'And what about the daughter, sir? Not bothering about her?'

Drew reflected and then tightened his lips.

'Not yet, anyway. See what develops. Now get out.'

4

Janet Kayne was surprised upon leaving the Drew Building that evening to find Jaline Quinton waiting for her in the street outside. The girl was pacing back and forth anxiously under the street lamps; then she came forward the moment she recognized the secretary's tall, bony figure.

'Oh, Miss Kayne. I've got to speak to you!'

'Of course,' Janet Kayne agreed. Then quietly, 'Is it still about your father?'

'Yes. He wasn't at the hotel when I got there and he hasn't come home yet. I'm perfectly certain that something happened to him, but I'm so at sea in this country I don't quite know what to do. Can you possibly help me?'

'I can try,' Janet Kayne said. 'There's a café a little further up the street. Suppose we talk over some tea?'

Jaline nodded urgently and they began

walking. It was perfectly clear to Janet Kayne that the Swiss girl wasn't far from hysteria in her anxiety. She kept repeating the same words over and over again, and when the bright lights of the café were upon her they showed up the pallor of her face and brightness of her eyes. It was obvious that she was undergoing an immense emotional strain.

'Now,' Janet Kayne said quietly, 'try and take things easy. Working yourself up won't do any good — not with a heart like yours. Here, drink some of this tea and try to settle down.'

Ruled for the moment by the other woman's stronger will Jaline obeyed, but when she had drunk her tea she started talking again in quick, jerky sentences.

'Yes, yes,' Janet Kayne said, nodding sympathetically, 'your father hasn't returned to the hotel and you've had no word from him since he left this morning. Asking Mr. Drew about it won't do any good since he is no wiser than you are. Your father left the building, and that's all we seem to know.'

'The funny thing is, though, that he left

in Mr. Drew's car,' Jaline said urgently.

'Oh? How do you know that?'

'While I was waiting for you this evening I asked the commissionaire and he distinctly remembers father leaving in Mr. Drew's car at ten to eleven this morning.'

Janet looked fixedly at her teacup, a hard light in her eyes and her lips tight.

'That's why I waited for you.' Jaline hurried on. 'I thought you could advise me what to do. Would it be possible to ask Mr. Drew's chauffeur where he left my father?'

An acid smile crossed the secretary's lips.

'Certainly it would be possible, but I don't recommend it. Brant — that's the chauffeur — is not the kind of man to tell anything he doesn't want you to know, and he's absolutely in Mr. Drew's confidence. I never met a man I distrusted more.'

'Then what am I to do?' Jaline demanded helplessly. 'I'm — I'm so lost in this city . . . Shall I tell the police?'

'I think,' Janet Kayne said slowly, 'we

ought to tell Scotland Yard. They represent the law in this country, Miss Quinton. And I'll tell you exactly why I suggest this course. As I told you, I am Mr. Drew's private secretary; I know a lot about him, and I tell you quite candidly I wouldn't trust him out of my sight for a moment. That is by the way — but I'm just recalling something that happened this morning. He was telephoning on the private wire to two of his greatest business friends, and incidentally two of the biggest commercial tycoons in the country — J. K. Darnhome and Marvin de Brock. You may not know of them, but I do.'

Jaline shook her head slowly.

'Mr. Drew said something about ' . . . the whole works' and 'It's all fixed up.' Then he arranged for Darnhome and de Brock to meet him tonight at his home. Now it seems to me that since this came right on top of your father handing over everything in connection with the bomb that there may be something grim going on.' Janet Kayne stopped, her lips thin and harsh. 'I know perfectly well that

I'm betraying my trust as private secretary,' she resumed calmly, 'but if there's some dirty work going on in connection with your father I don't give a hoot for confidences. I've only got the slimmest of clues, of course, but Scotland Yard might be interested. Certainly we have got to do something.'

'How do I get to Scotland Yard?' Jaline asked anxiously.

'I'll take you there,' Janet Kayne said, signaling the waiter for the check. 'Come along.'

They left the café together and in ten minutes were walking along Whitehall. It was not easy to gain permission to see Chief Inspector Poole of the C.I.D., but finally Janet Kayne's impersonal woman-of-the-world manner broke down the barrier and the two women were ushered into the Inspector's office by a Sergeant.

Aware over the interphone of the bare details, Poole greeted them cordially enough.

'Good evening, ladies.' He was a short, rotund man with tumbled brown hair and a genial smile. 'Do sit down, please.' He drew up chairs and then stood beside the desk contemplating them in the bright light. 'Five minutes later and I would have been on my way home,' he said. 'Now, what's the trouble? I believe you said somebody was missing?'

'Yes, sir — my father,' Jaline said urgently, and at a nod from the secretary went into the details.

Chief Inspector Poole listened without interrupting, returning to his chair at the other side of the desk and sinking his chin on to his hand.

'I see,' he said finally. 'Pardon me a moment — '

He pressed a switch on the interphone box and spoke briefly.

'Have Mr. Clark come in here, will you, please? I don't think he'll have left for home yet.'

Poole switched off again and there was a brief silence in the office. Then a youngish man in the mid-thirties entered — tall, broad-shouldered, even handsome after a fashion. His hair was black, his eyes blue. A man more unlike a police official would have been hard to discover.

'Sent for me, Chief?' he enquired, glancing at the two women.

'Yes, Larry. Sit down, please. I'd like you to hear something. This is Miss Quinton — and Miss Kayne. Mr. Clark is in our department, ladies.'

There were mutual smiles of acknowledgement and Larry Clark seated himself at the desk, waiting. Poole eased his bulky figure into a more comfortable position.

'Sorry as I am to bother you, Miss Quinton, I'd be glad if you would repeat to Mr. Clark here the story you just told me. Every detail.'

Jaline nodded and did as asked. Clark listened attentively, making a note now and again on the scratchpad beside him, then when the girl had finished he glanced at the Chief Inspector.

'Might be something — or nothing,' he commented. 'We can start an enquiry, of course, but there's nothing tangible to go on.'

'That, gentlemen, is where you're mistaken,' Janet Kayne said briefly. 'As I've said, I am private secretary to Mr. Drew. It is a responsible position, a

58

confidential one, and I'm relying on the fact that whatever I say here won't get back to him. I heard Mr. Drew calling both Mr. Darnhome and Mr. de Brock this morning on the private wire and . . . Well, his words sounded significant, now I come to think back upon them.'

'What were the words?' the Chief Inspector asked.

Janet Kayne repeated them and Poole rubbed his chin.

'So,' he said, pondering, 'it appears that Mr. Quinton had an invention of extreme value, handed it over to Emerson Drew in return for a signed receipt, or undertaking, was then driven away from the building in Drew's car and has not been seen since. On top of that Drew telephones to two of the biggest industrialists in the country remarking on something being 'all fixed up' and that they had got 'the whole works.' Very, very slim evidence, Miss Quinton — Miss Kayne. Naturally, we cannot accuse either Emerson Drew or his chauffeur with such flimsy stuff at the back of us. On the other hand, people cannot be allowed to mysteriously disappear. I'd suggest you leave this in our hands for the moment and we'll make enquiries.'

'You can't do any more than that?' Jaline asked worriedly.

'Unfortunately, no, Miss Quinton.' Poole gave her a sympathetic smile. 'I can quite understand your anxiety, but try and have patience. Now, tell me, you say your father has fifty thousand pounds in large denomination notes in one of the trunks in his room?'

'That's right, yes.'

'But isn't it risky?'

'I suppose so,' Jaline admitted. 'In fact it is, and I've reproached him for it. But — but what has that to do with him disappearing, Inspector?'

'I'm not sure,' Poole replied, musing. 'But there is the possibility that his disappearance may not have anything to do with Drew at all — namely, that some thieves have got to know about his fifty thousand in the trunk — and you'd be surprised how such news does get around sometimes — and have abducted him. If that is the case you will perhaps receive a ransom note before long asking for the fifty thousand in return for your father. I repeat, it is a possibility, particularly as your father happens to be a most important inventor whose life, to thieves anyway, is worth fifty thousand any day.'

Jaline's face had gone a little paler at the suggestion.

'So I repeat,' Poole said, 'just leave it to us.'

With that both women had to he satisfied and they left the office with Poole's handshakes. When he had closed the door his expression changed. Hands deep in his jacket pockets he strolled towards the desk, brows down.

'It smells nasty, Chief,' Larry Clark commented, musing.

'Of course it's nasty! The whole damned thing's perfectly obvious. Drew's arranged it so that Quinton has handed over an invention of immense value — which in any case is contrary to the existing laws regarding the control of atomic energy — and has wiped out the inventor after fleecing him of every secret he's got. I don't have to tell you that

61

Drew has been suspect ever since the unexplained disappearances of Travers of New York and L'Estrage of Paris. Both those men had dealings with Drew, but Drew's too wily to be nabbed. This, though, may be our chance.'

'How do we go about it? We may suspect Drew — just as much as we suspect the machinations of those two tycoons de Brock and Darnhome — but we can't accuse any of them to their faces. No proof for one thing and they're a darned sight too powerful for another.'

'I know it,' Poole growled. 'The fact remains, this begins to look like murder — just as in the case of L'Estrage and Travers. At the moment the trail is pretty hot since Quinton has only just disappeared. It starts with the chauffeur, who'd only lie his way out of it if we questioned him, and it ends with — Well, that's for you to find out.'

Larry Clark raised an eyebrow. 'I? Well, I'm not dashing at it, let me tell you.'

'Look here, Larry, you're one of the best men in the Special Branch when it comes to being a good mixer — and that isn't flattery but plain commonsense. You're going to start on this Quinton job right away, not as a detective but as a man-about-town. Spend all you like and *do* what you like, but somehow get yourself into Drew's confidence and get us the proof we need to convict him — and if possible those other two men who always seem to work with him.'

Larry Clark got to his feet and gave a rueful smile.

'All right; you're the doctor. When do I start?'

'Tonight. And you have *carte blanche*. Men like Drew are not a menace to just a *few* people but to millions. If that secret is left with Drew, God knows what sort of international repercussions there may be. You've got the looks and the brains — so go to it!'

★ ★ ★

Towards eleven o'clock the following morning Emerson Drew's interphone buzzed sharply. With an irritable movement he put down his pen and pressed the switch.

63

'Well?'

Janet Kayne's clear voice answered him. 'There's Miss Quinton here to see you, sir.'

'Miss Quinton?' Drew frowned and reflected swiftly. 'What does she want?'

'She won't say, sir. She says it is a private matter.'

'All right; show her in.'

Drew sat back in his chair and waited, but as Jaline Quinton was shown into the office, ghost-faced and weary-looking, the financier got to his feet and extended a cordial hand. Janet Kayne retired and closed the door.

'Good morning, Miss Quinton — I'm glad to know you. Though I won't add that this is a surprise.'

The girl ignored the extended hand and the chair to which Drew motioned. Instead she stood looking at him levelly with her blue eyes. A small hat framed the blonde of her hair.

'This won't take very long, Mr. Drew,' she said. 'I'm here to settle an account . . . '

Abruptly a .32 revolver was in her hand, taken from the large bag she was carrying. Drew's eyes lowered to it and his mouth set hard.

'What's the idea?' he asked briefly, raising his eyes back to her face.

'I know you've killed my father!' The girl spoke now a dead, flat monotone. 'He's not been seen since he left here in your car yesterday morning. Scotland Yard knows the facts — the time he left, that he went in your car, and they knew you are trying to share his secret with two men called Darnhome and de Brock. They want proof — but I don't. I'm prepared to settle matters here and now!'

Drew continued to stare at her; the dead-white face, the steady hand. It struck him as surprising for a moment that such a slender, wispy-looking girl should have such courage. Then he grinned widely.

'Now just a minute, young woman: you're letting your imagination run away with you! I know your father has disappeared, of course, because it's in the morning papers — but that's no reason for thinking that I did it. A man with an invention as valuable as your father's might have dozens of enemies, both British and European.'

'You can't evade it that way,' Jaline answered coldly. '*You* are the cause of his disappearance and, as I now believe, his death.' A taut, bitter smile crossed her face. 'This gun I have is one that he always left with me for protection. But that is no reason why it can't be used for vengeance, too.'

Drew hesitated — then as swiftly as the head of a striking snake he brought his fist down on the girl's hand and knocked the revolver spinning before she could fire it. He snatched it up from the floor, emptied it, then handed it back to her.

'I'd advise you to get out of this office, Miss Quinton,' he said grimly. 'I could have you arrested for this — and if you dare to come back again I shall. You'll realize later, when your father turns up with quite a reasonable explanation, how foolish you've been.'

'What about that invention of his?' the girl demanded, her coldness breaking down into something bordering on tears. 'You just *can't* keep it now he's vanished!'

'Why not?' Drew asked briefly. 'There's no guarantee that he has vanished for good: in fact he'll probably come back just as suddenly. Until he does so, possession is nine points of the law. I'll bid you good morning, Miss Quinton.'

He snatched the office door open for her and held it. She hesitated, put the revolver back in her handbag, then went out without another word. Set-faced, Drew closed the door and went across to his desk, snapped on the interphone.

'Miss Kayne!' His voice was sharp as a blade-edge. 'Come in here at once!'

'With my notebook, sir?'

'No!'

Drew switched off, plunged his hands in his pockets and stood waiting, the corners of his mouth drawn, cold fury in his gray eyes. Janet Kayne entered as quietly as ever and closed the door.

'I thought,' Drew said, with vicious calm, 'that you were my personal and private secretary?'

Janet Kayne, by no means insensitive to the gathering storm, held her ground. Her level eyes looked back across the desk.

'I have endeavored to fill that position, sir, yes,' she agreed calmly.

'Like hell you have!' Drew snatched a fist out of his pocket and banged it on the desk. 'You were talking to that Quinton girl yesterday dinner time; I saw you as I went through the hall. Now I find out that you have been telling her private business. Haven't you got the damned sense to know that whatever happens in this office, or in this concern for that matter, is strictly, implicitly private?'

The steel nerves of Janet Kayne did not let her down. She waited with perfect composure even though her face did seem to go a shade paler.

'I could understand better, Mr. Drew, if you'd explain what you mean?'

'All right, I will!' He glared at her. 'Miss Quinton is upset by the disappearance of her father. She's taken the matter up with Scotland Yard, and I can't blame her for that. But she also told Scotland Yard some cock-and-bull story about my sharing Quinton's secret with Mr. de Brock and Mr. Darnhome. She could not possibly have known about them unless you had told her. You were in here yesterday when I telephoned them. Just what right had you to pass that information on?'

Janet Kayne gave a cold, thin smile.

'Mr. Drew, I am a woman who tries to live up to certain principles. Much that you do is no concern of mine, and in general I never divulge what happens in this office — but in this case I made an exception. I believe that Mr. Quinton has been coldly and brutally murdered — or otherwise disposed of, and that you have stolen his secret and intend to share it with the only two men who can possibly make use of it. For that reason I allowed Scotland Yard to know everything I could — and in the same circumstances I'd do it again! I have no intention of condoning murder, not even for the purpose of respecting business confidence.'

'You realize I can have you jailed for this?' Drew snapped.

'Yes — if there had been witnesses to my words. Since there have not you're just wasting your time, Mr. Drew. In any case, even if you did clap me in jail, I wouldn't mind. The truth has been told, as far as I know it, and it will take cleverer men than you, de Brock and Darnhome to beat Scotland Yard.'

Drew's lips twitched. The girl's placid eyes, cold with disgust, were fixed on him.

'I'm not a fool, Mr. Drew,' she finished quietly. 'I know perfectly well that the mysterious fates of L'Estrage of Paris and Travers of New York can probably be laid at your door. In so far as Quinton is concerned I'm convinced of it. I did my utmost to dissuade Miss Quinton from seeing you, but I just couldn't manage it — '

'In case she talked and revealed what you had said, of course?'

'Certainly,' Janet Kayne agreed. 'I didn't want you to know if I could help it. The longer you remained in ignorance the more I might have been able to find out about you.'

Drew gestured to the .32 bullets lying on his desk.

'That woman held me up with a gun. I suppose you didn't know anything about that, either?'

'No, I didn't. Jaline Quinton is a somewhat impulsive girl, and acts without thinking — '

'One thing is pretty certain — you don't!' Drew sneered. 'And from this moment, Miss Kayne, you are no longer employed here. Get your salary to date from the cashier's department and leave.'

'I demand a further month's salary in lieu of notice. I know my rights.'

'Very well. Tell the cashier.'

Janet Kayne turned and left. Angry or otherwise she closed the door as quietly as ever. Drew stood glaring at it for a moment and then snapped on an interphone switch.

'Brant? Listen — there's something I want you to do, and do it now . . . '

While Drew gave his instructions Jaline Quinton was walking slowly and wearily along the high street outside. She had no eyes for the people passing to and fro; her thoughts were entirely on the passage-at-arms she had had with Drew. Nor, now the reaction of her visit was telling upon her, did she feel particularly steady. She had been calm enough at the time, but that deadly pain was biting in her chest again and a sense of giddiness was clamping down upon her.

She looked up, took a grip on herself, and tried to ignore the symptoms pressing upon her. Then suddenly, ahead of her, her attention became fixed on a medium-sized figure. He was badly-dressed, slouching along, had one arm crooked as he held a handkerchief to his face. There was something about the walk, about the bend of the shoulders, that was instantly familiar.

'*Dad* . . . ' Jaline whispered incredulously. 'Oh — dad!'

Forgetting everything else she broke into a run, bundling past the surprised people who dodged out of her way. Faster she ran after the figure, and faster still, before he could be lost in the crowd —

'*Dad*!' she screamed hoarsely — and as she ran she felt the pain in her chest tightening. The world seemed to be spinning round in wild circles and there was a monstrous roaring in her ears.

5

When Janet Kayne left the Drew Building half an hour after her altercation with the financier she did not go immediately to her flat. Instead she lunched at a small café, and then went on to the public library to search through the daily papers for a new post. The sooner she found one, the better. She had enough money to last for perhaps six months, but living on her capital, as she well knew, was the sure road to ruin.

Altogether her search occupied a full hour, then with three potential openings jotted down she left the library and began to walk down the side streets in the direction of Pennistone Gate, her first point of contact.

She was not immediately aware of a powerful car following her at a distance. It only began to impress itself on her notice as she turned into the quiet length of Barraclough Street — a long deserted vista flanked on either side by granaries. Here there was dirty yellow sunshine and the smell of straw, complete with that dreary absence of life which invests so many slum by-roads.

The quiet and desertion aroused her attention to the dull purring of a car engine which had been with her for some time now. Puzzled, she glanced up — then behind her. It took her five seconds to realize that the shining bonnet of Emerson Drew's Chrysler was nearby. She could not see the face of the driver behind the reflections on the windscreen but she had little doubt but that it was Douglas Brant.

Immediately she broke into a run, the premonition of deadly danger hard upon her. Anything — anywhere — An open doorway — a deserted office — a side street — But in this long, dreary length there were no such escapes.

She ran, and harder still, her heels clicking on the empty pavement and behind her the purring engine suddenly rose to a surge of power. She stopped, swung round, screamed as her nerves gave way —

The monstrous bonnet was plunging straight at her, bumpers gleaming. She flattened against the wall, arms outspread in a helpless gesture . . .

Towards four o'clock that afternoon Larry Clark entered the office of Chief Inspector Poole and found him busy at his desk. Detective-Sergeant Jones was typing on a noiseless machine at a table near the window.

'Hello, Larry,' Poole greeted. 'I was wondering if you'd be dropping in. How are you fixed?'

Larry Clark seated himself at the desk. 'I dropped in to tell you that I'm fixed up with a flat in Mayfair — and at a rent that is going to raise questions as well as eyebrows if I don't get some good results to justify it. I'm under the name of Peter Maxton and you can always get me on the private line there. I've taken Calvert along to act as my manservant. He's a good man. You wanted me to become a man-about-town and I've done it.'

Poole noted the particulars down and nodded.

'Okay. Anything else? Any contacts yet?'

'No contacts, but there's something in the first edition of the *Evening Standard* that may interest you — ' Larry pulled the issue out of his pocket and read — ' "The body of a woman, since identified by articles in her handbag as Janet Kayne of Villiers Crescent, London, was found this afternoon by granary workmen. The body was lying on the pavement in Barraclough Street, S.E. The woman had apparently been crushed to death by a motor vehicle: If anybody has any information — ' and so on.'

Larry stopped, his good-looking face harshly set. Poole was nodding slowly.

'Yes,' he said, in a quiet voice. 'I know. We got the report half an hour ago. Suppose you tell me what we can do about it? Absolutely nothing! The whole thing was apparently a hit-and-run act. We can assume that Drew arranged it — and that Brant did it; but we can't prove it. We're bogged down by the old bugbear of the 'reasonable doubt.' We haven't even enough to drag Brant in for questioning.'

'There's something else in the paper

that makes me think it is Drew's doing,' Larry added, turning the pages. 'Yes, listen to this: 'Vacant Situations' column — Required by the Drew Financial Corporation, a personal and private secretary. Highest references required and a knowledge of foreign languages essential. High remuneration. Call personally between eleven and twelve tomorrow — Wednesday morning.'

'That,' Poole agreed, 'is our answer. The thing links up. I rather thought when Miss Kayne was here last night that she was letting the cat a long way out of the secretarial bag. Obviously Drew thought so too, fired her, and to make sure she talked no more he . . . '

Poole spread his hands eloquently and then planted them on the desk.

'I was wondering,' Larry said slowly, 'if it wouldn't be good idea if *I* applied for that job? I might be lucky and it would save a lot of trouble. It doesn't say man or woman and I can speak several languages fluently.'

'Good idea,' Poole agreed. 'By this time Drew probably knows that we are trying to pin something on him, but I can't see that that should make him suspect you. He'll be pretty ruthless in his questioning, though. Sure your tracks are well covered?'

'Certain. I've even arranged for a family tree.'

'I knew I picked the right man,' Poole smiled.

Larry folded the paper, put it back in his pocket and thought for a moment. 'Look here, Chief, how about this woman Janet Kayne? What are you going to do — let Drew get away with it?'

'For the moment I have to. Only you can get the evidence we need, both in regard to Janet Kayne and Quinton. The body will be taken to the mortuary, an inquest will be held, and I'll bet my boots the verdict will be 'Death from Misadventure' or something of that order. Nothing we can do there at the moment, Larry . . . However,' Poole went on, 'I haven't been idle while you've been getting yourself 'domiciled.' I made enquiries at the Grand Hotel this morning where Quinton and his daughter have been staying; I also took a search warrant to examine their rooms. I discovered something rather odd . . . '

Larry Clark looked up expectantly.

'Last night Miss Quinton told me that her father had fifty thousand pounds put away in his trunk — his entire monetary possessions. I questioned the wisdom of such a course. However, that's by the way. The significant thing is that the fifty thousand is nowhere in those hotel rooms — Quinton's or his daughter's. And as you know we don't miss much when we search. The money has gone, yet nothing else has been touched.'

'Thieves?' Larry suggested. 'More than possible that Jaline had let the facts about the money slip out somewhere, and in an hotel that's asking for it.'

'Possible, yes,' Poole admitted, frowning. 'Clever thieves, too, because the door locks were untouched. It even looks as if whoever did it had a key. The other odd thing is that Miss Quinton left the hotel this morning and has not been seen since. Of course she may be in town somewhere, but as I understood it last night she doesn't usually stray far, being unaccustomed to the city. I'm beginning to wonder, Larry,' Poole finished slowly, 'if she too has vanished like her father! I've left instructions with the hotel to notify me the moment she turns up again. I want to ask her one or two more questions.'

Larry Clark pondered for a moment or two.

'Do you know if either of them took their door keys away with them — girl or father? People do that sometimes.'

'I asked about it. The girl left hers at her desk when she went out; that's how I know what time she left. But it seems that Quinton took his with him when he set off yesterday morning to see Drew. Understandable — the excitement, and being a bit of a preoccupied sort of chap anyway. Why? What's the significance?'

'I was just wondering — Quinton has a key and the rooms — one of them anyway — have been entered without leaving traces. Supposing Quinton isn't dead after all?'

'But it doesn't make sense!' Poole protested. 'For one thing he would be instantly recognized. For another, why should he just take his money and leave everything else behind? Why keep silent when he must have a story good enough to blow the Drew Corporation wide open? No, I don't agree with you there, Larry. I'm pretty sure he's dead.'

Larry got to his feet.

'Well, maybe that's the way it is. Anyhow, I'll do what I can from now on — and let me know if anything develops at the hotel. I'll advise you what happens about the secretary's job.'

Poole nodded. 'I'll leave it to you, Larry — and whatever help or equipment you need don't forget to ask for it.'

'As if I would!' Larry grinned, and headed for the door.

* * *

At eleven o'clock the following morning Larry Clark entered the Drew Building, perfectly dressed, carrying a briefcase full of 'credentials' — looking, in fact, the perfect man-about-town.

He had left his Mayfair flat not very

long before, in possession of the information over the private wire from the Yard that Jaline Quinton had not yet returned to the hotel. Like her father, she seemed to have completely disappeared. If the news did nothing else it stiffened Larry's determination to get workable facts on which to build a case against Emerson Drew.

Entering the reception office and making his business known to the girl at the desk he found himself conducted into an anteroom. There was only one other person present — a well-dressed girl in a gray two-piece, her blonde hair bushing from under a saucy hat.

As Larry entered she was reclining in one of the armchairs, glancing through a magazine. Her eyes, hidden by densely thick spectacles, rose to look at him.

'Mr. Drew won't be very long now,' the reception clerk said, and retired.

Larry took a chair almost facing the reclining girl. Unobtrusively his eyes went down the small, slender lines of her figure to the well-shaped legs and neat shoes. He guessed her age at about twenty-six.

He liked the roundness of her chin and the straightness of her nose. What color her eyes were it was impossible to tell.

He coughed quietly to himself, picked up a magazine and scanned idly through it. Then his gaze strayed to the girl's briefcase at the side of her chair. Finally he put his magazine down and sighed.

'Do you think Mr. Drew is likely to be long?' he asked.

The spectacles focused on him again as the girl raised her head. Slender shoulders shrugged imperceptibly.

'I'm sure I don't know. I've been waiting fifteen minutes and nothing's happened yet.'

'A habit of these big men,' Larry commented, grinning. 'To keep people waiting conveys an air of importance. I'll bet two to one he's practicing golf strokes in the office or something.'

He could not be sure of it, but it looked as if the girl were studying him. Not that it mattered if she were. He knew, without a vestige of conceit, that he was good-looking, young, and broad in the shoulder. The only thing about the girl that annoyed him was the impenetrability, not to say the ugliness, of her spectacles.

'Er — if I'm not being too personal — ' He hesitated. 'Are you applying for the secretary's post?'

'I am, yes.'

'So am I. I'm overstuffed with credentials in this case of mine.'

'I've little doubt,' the girl said, 'that I can give you a run for your money. There doesn't seem to be anybody else but you and me for it.'

'Probably the need of several languages is a stumbling block to most applicants. I suppose you speak them?'

'Seven of them like a native.' The girl smiled to reveal even teeth. 'I hope I didn't sound too hostile towards you just now when I said I'd give you a run for your money. I didn't mean it that way. It's just that I'm going to put all I can into my application because I — I need the money, badly.'

'If it comes to that, what makes you think I don't?'

'Well, of course . . . ' She shrugged. 'Maybe you do; but speaking selfishly I'm glad I'll be interviewed before you.'

Larry relaxed and smiled, considering her.

'I've a pretty good notion to walk out of here this moment. Coming after you I won't stand a chance. Most big business men prefer lady secretaries. You look the part. Unfortunately for me my background sticks out all over me. Money, no real need to work for a living — until now. Things are not what they were any more, for me. Incidentally, my name is Peter Maxton.'

'I'm glad to know you, Mr. Maxton. I'm Joyce Sutton.' Larry got to his feet and shook her hand as she extended it. Then he proffered his cigarette case.

'Not now, thanks — hardly do.'

He reflected. 'Mmm — maybe you're right. Perhaps — later?'

She did not answer, but he fancied her eyes were blue. The lenses made them seem far smaller than they really were. Altogether, she was pretty good-looking.

'I think — ' Larry started to say; then the office door opened.

'Mr. Drew will see you now, Miss

Sutton. Will you come this way?'

The girl nodded and got to her feet, picking up her briefcase. Larry noticed with satisfaction that she was not very tall — no more than five feet three.

Following the reception clerk into the corridor Joyce Sutton found herself ushered into the huge private office where Emerson Drew was pacing slowly up and down, biting on his cigar.

'Miss — er — Sutton?' he asked, glancing down at the card on his desk. 'Take a seat, please.'

The girl obeyed and laid her briefcase in her lap. For moment or two Drew continued his pacing, appraising her from various angles. Then —

'What are your qualifications for this post, Miss Sutton? And sum them up as briefly as you can, please.'

'Five years as a clerk with the British Chemical Corporation.'

'Uh-huh. Why did you leave?'

'I didn't consider the salary sufficient and when they refused to higher it I walked out.'

'A woman of independent notions, eh?'

Drew grinned briefly as he made notes on his scratchpad. 'What do you expect to get here for remuneration?'

The girl named a figure — a high one. 'That's just a starting salary, of course. I'd expect it to rise if I'm satisfactory.'

Drew said nothing. Money was no problem to him. His cold gray eyes were still pondering her.

'I take it you can speak several languages? Let me hear you.'

Joyce Sutton reeled off sentence after sentence in various tongues and Drew nodded pensively.

'Good! And shorthand and typing skills, of course?'

'Yes; but I hardly think much of that should fall to my lot, as personal secretary.'

'Not much, no — but some.' Drew half-perched on the desk, his eyes fixed on her. 'What is your background, Miss Sutton? Whom and what are your parents? Alive or dead? I want a brief resumé of your life and upbringing.'

'Is that really — important, sir?' the girl asked quietly.

'Very. I might as well tell you that I have to know every detail about my private secretary because she will have to be entrusted with many secrets. I can't take too many precautions. If you don't feel like giving me the facts, suppose we forget about the whole thing, eh?'

'I'll give them,' the girl said quietly. 'Born in London 26 years ago — educated at Wyecombe College; trained for the Civil Service but didn't care for it. Took my position as clerk with British Chemicals two years after I had left school and was there until a month ago. My parents are dead, and I'm unmarried.'

'Are you engaged?'

'No, Mr. Drew.'

'That's a good thing. I prefer my private secretary to have no close attachments with anybody.' Drew put down his pencil again from note taking. 'This next question is personal, and I can't compel you to answer it — but it will influence me a lot making my decision. What is the matter with your eyesight?'

'Well, nothing really: that is, nothing

permanent. When I was with British Chemicals I got mixed up one day in the fumes of some gas and it affected my eyes — weakened them a lot. But the oculist says it will pass off in a few more months. Until then I have to wear these. But you don't have to worry whether I see well or not. I do — with these on.'

'I wasn't thinking of that, Miss Sutton: I was just thinking that without your glasses you might remind me of somebody. Would you object to taking them off for a moment?'

The girl felt behind her ears and took the spectacles away. Drew gazed solemnly into her steady blue eyes, studied her face intently with its delicately-pink cheeks. Finally he gazed at her hair. Then he nodded.

'All right. Thank you for doing as I asked: I have to be sure.' He straightened up from the desk. 'Naturally you have all the necessary credentials?'

'Everything — including language diplomas.' Joyce Sutton unfastened the briefcase and set the various documents out on the desk. 'I'll leave them for the moment if you wish: There are quite a number of them and you'll want to verify them.'

'To the hilt,' Drew agreed. 'As I have said, this job is most confidential. I will say, though, that you have impressed me very favorably, Miss Sutton. Call back again at this time tomorrow for my decision, will you?'

She nodded and got to her feet. Going ahead of her, Drew opened the door — then he glanced at Larry in the anteroom beyond.

'You applying for this position, young man?'

'Er — yes, Mr. Drew. I thought — '

'I'm sorry, but you're wasting your time. I don't employ male secretaries: they aren't tractable enough. My clerk did not tell me why you were here. Good day, Miss Sutton; see you tomorrow.'

The door closed and Larry gave a faintly rueful smile.

'Well, nothing like knowing where you stand,' he sighed, picking up his case. 'I don't think I've ever been turned down so quickly in my life! How did you make out, Miss Sutton?'

'I rather think I've got the job. I satisfied him on every point. I'm coming back tomorrow at this time to find out. I'm sorry I've done you out of it, though.'

Larry regarded the girl's serious face.

'But you haven't. It's just as I said — he'd never take a man like me when he could have a girl like you. Wouldn't be natural, now would it?'

She smiled but did not comment. Larry held the door open for her and they went out into the corridor together. He walked with her as far as the elevator.

'Do you think,' he ventured, 'you'd care to be revived over a cup of coffee, Miss Sutton?'

'Why not?'

Larry nodded and followed her into the elevator. In five minutes they were seated at a table in the Pyramid Café, a block away from the Drew Building.

'Just one thing in this whole business puzzles me,' Joyce said, pondering. 'Mr. Drew seemed frightfully concerned over the fact that I reminded him of somebody. He even made me take off my glasses as though to satisfy himself. Whom do you imagine he could have been thinking of?'

'I've no idea,' Larry replied, shrugging; then after a moment or two's thought he added, 'I don't quite know how you take this, Miss Sutton — but I wouldn't consider I was playing fair if I didn't tell you about it. Do you know whom Drew's last secretary was? The one before you?'

The girl shook her blonde head negatively.

'Her name was Janet Kayne. She was found dead yesterday afternoon, the victim of a hit-and-run motorist.'

Joyce drank the remainder of her coffee and set the cup down.

'I read about that in the papers — but of course I didn't know she had been Drew's secretary.' The dense lenses turned to face Larry. 'What are you trying to do, Mr. Maxton? Scare me off, or something?'

'Not a bit of it; I'm just pointing out facts. Janet Kayne *might* have been the victim of an accident, of course; we don't know. But I *do* know that she was dismissed before she met the accident, and not afterwards. That is, she had been fired and then was knocked down: I know that because the advertisement for a new secretary must have been handed in to the paper before she died. I've wondered since if she perhaps — er — talked out of turn.'

'Well, if she did that it was her own fault. I'm not the nervous type, Mr. Maxton. If I can get this position I can look after myself well enough — but thanks for considering my interests.' The girl paused and reflected. 'You seem to know a lot about Drew and his activities? How does that come about?'

Larry grinned. 'Oh, I move about in fairly high circles. I get to hear things. I do want a job, though — somehow. I've a Mayfair flat to keep going and money is running out fast; that which the old man left me. I'll find something — somewhere. If nothing else comes out of my efforts I have at least met you and I count that as worth a good deal.'

'Do you? It's nice of you to say it.'

'I'd like to continue our friendship — if you're willing?'

'One doesn't meet a person every day who can speak several languages,' the girl commented dryly.

'One language will do me, for all I have to say. You'll be free tonight, won't you? How about the Majestic? There's a good play on there . . . '

Joyce Sutton was nodding slowly. Then she laughed.

'All right; why not?'

'Good!' Larry rubbed his hands. 'I'll pick you up in my car at six-thirty tonight.'

'That'll be fine. But you don't know my address.'

'I shall do when I've taken you home after lunch.'

6

Towards the middle of the afternoon Douglas Brant entered Drew's office and walked across to the desk briskly. Drew looked up from his work enquiringly.

'Well? Find out anything?'

'Everything, Mr. Drew. Every word that girl uttered seems to be true. I even went down to Wyecombe to that school she used to go to, and it's right; she was there at one time. And she *did* work at British Chemicals and get her eyes mixed up with fumes. That was one reason why she left, apart from salary trouble. I used my special approach — navy blue suit and insurance investigator angle.'

'Hmmm . . . ' Drew meditated and jabbed his pen javelin-wise at the blotter. 'It's a bit of a surprise to me. You know, that girl Joyce Sutton looks enough like Jaline Quinton to be her sister — if she had one. Similar hair, eyes, and slender build. There *are* differences, of course

— color in the cheeks, hairstyle, and voice. But all those things could be altered without much effort. I was so sure there was some trick that I had her take her glasses off. It occurred to me that Joyce Sutton might be Jaline in disguise, trying on some stunt.'

Brant shook his bullet head.

'Afraid you're wrong this time, Mr. Drew. I don't see how any girl could fake credentials which go back for years — especially one like Jaline Quinton who's new to the city.'

'You're probably right,' Drew admitted, rubbing his chin. 'Just a similarity of appearance which made me suspicious. Okay, I'm satisfied. I'll give her the job. Incidentally, you've kept tabs on the Grand Hotel? The Quinton girl returned there yet?'

'According to Billy, no.'

'Billy?' Drew frowned. 'Who in hell's Billy?'

Brant grinned. 'Just one of my contacts, sir. He's a bell-boy at the Grand and covers anything I want to know. One of the boys on your unofficial pay-roll.'

'Hmm! So she hasn't returned, eh? I just can't understand where she's gone to — which was one reason why I suspected this Sutton girl.' Drew seemed to make up his mind suddenly. 'All right, you can go. You can take a couple of hours off to make up for the time you've put in. I shan't be leaving until five.'

Brant nodded and went out, humming a tune to himself. Downstairs he climbed into the Chrysler standing at the kerb and then pondered for a moment. It was too late for a drink, but not for an hour of poker at Joe Clanston's place. Pass the time on, and it offered a chance of some money on the side. Brant nodded to himself and, starting the car up, began to thread through the traffic carefully. He had been progressing smoothly for perhaps five minutes when something hard prodded in the back of his neck just above the collar. It was something icy cold too, which sent a shiver down him.

'Just keep on driving, Brant! I'll direct you!'

'What the devil — ' Brant half-turned — then he jerked his eyes to the front again as a car swept across his path.

'Keep your eyes on the road,' the voice ordered — measured, deadly.

Brant breathed hard and felt perspiration suddenly run down the sides of his face. He knew that voice, despite its present relentless monotone. It had belonged to Rajek Quinton. It *did* belong to Rajek Quinton. That was the impossibility of it! Brant's eyes flashed to the rear mirror but all he could see was the top of a gray soft hat as his traveling companion kept well down, one hand holding an automatic embedded now at the very top of Brant's spine.

'One move the wrong way, Brant, and I'll finish you,' the voice whispered. 'Drive as fast as you can to the spot where you took me yesterday.'

'But — but you can't be Quinton!' Brant gasped out.

'I *am* Quinton — and keep going!'

Dazed though he was Brant obeyed, making his way through the traffic with the hard muzzle of the automatic pressing into him. No further words reached him until he had driven to the same spot as yesterday with the props of the disused mine shaft visible across the deserted fields.

'Get out!' the voice snapped. 'And keep your hands up!'

Brant obeyed and the man at the back of the car slid out silently and confronted him. For a moment Brant's brain got a jolt. It was hardly possible to tell that the ruined face did indeed belong to Rajek Quinton. Hideous burns were across it, only half-healed. Wadding was taped down one side of it. A blistered mouth was set in a thin, inflexible line. Eyes rendered intense by the eyebrows and lashes having been scorched away, glared at Brant mesmerically.

'Yes — you're Quinton,' Brant whispered: 'Only I — I hardly recognized you. But you couldn't have got out of that mine! You just couldn't have — '

'But I did — and I'm here.' Quinton still stared, his burned hand holding the gun. 'Luckily for me you weren't as straight in aiming that acid as you could have been. I saved my eyes anyway, by throwing up my hands in time — but I couldn't save my lashes and my face, or my hands. I haven't forgotten what you did to me, Brant. No, by God, I haven't forgotten.'

'But look, Quinton. I was only acting under orders. You've got to believe that!'

'I fell in that mine quagmire face down,' Quinton went on, as though he had never been interrupted. 'It didn't smother me; my feet and hands just reached across it, on to the firm sides. The wet took a great deal of the acid off my face. I was dazed, but not dead. I climbed out, my clothes rotting. There were, and still are, iron footrests down the shaft sides. Half a mile from here is a cottage. I got that far and then collapsed. The good people of the cottage patched me up and sent for a doctor. I told them a tale about a car battery exploding in my face. I didn't give anything away. I want to keep all this to myself. But I put you down on my list as Number One!'

Brant's eyes stared frozenly. 'I keep on telling you Quinton — I only do as I'm told!'

'I have only one regret,' Quinton

continued. 'I haven't any acid with me with which to repay you — but I do have this automatic. I've carried it about with me for years and never had a need to use it: but now I can make up for it! I waited my chance to get you alone, coming out of the Drew Building. When you left the car outside I climbed into the back and covered myself with the rug as it lay on the floor. I waited. Had Drew come down the building steps with you I'd have had plenty of chance to escape — but he didn't. You were alone — just as we are alone now.'

Quinton stopped and took a deep breath.

'Start walking, Brant,' he ordered quietly.

Brant, his hands still raised, took a stumbling step backwards; then suddenly his expression changed. His hands lowered in a sudden blur of action and he lunged.

Quinton jerked himself to one side and fired — twice. Brant staggered and clutched his shoulder painfully.

'I'm not dealing with you all at once,' Quinton said implacably. 'I want you to enjoy this. Now *walk*, damn you!'

The violent shove he received sent Brant staggering forward again over the uneven ground. In any case there was nothing he could do now to help himself. His right arm was paralyzed, with blood from the shoulder wound already seeping between the clenching fingers of his left hand as he held it over the injury. Dazed, he came at last to the edge of the mineshaft.

'Quinton, for God's sake — !' he implored desperately.

Quinton's hideous face did not alter its expression. He fired deliberately — three times. Brant felt each bullet tear into his body and staggered backwards, clutching at empty space. With a final helpless scream he slipped over the edge of the shaft and vanished from sight.

Quinton put the automatic inside his coat and climbed over the edge of the mine, went down footrest by footrest, into the depths. When he came up again, the cruel mouth was smiling. He drew his coat a little tighter about him and strode off across the field.

Emerson Drew was in the library of his London home that evening when the police sergeant was shown in to him. The sergeant hesitated a moment at the sight of the two men with the financier — de Brock and Darnhome — but Drew waved his hand impatiently.

'All right, Sergeant, say what you've got to say. Have you found my car and chauffeur, or haven't you?'

'Yes, sir, we've got your car. I've just given orders for it to be driven into the garage here. We found it on the West Fork road on the way to Godalming. Abandoned. P.C. Pascall discovered it about half past seven this evening after you'd reported its loss and the disappearance of your chauffeur. We — '

'What *about* my chauffeur?' Drew snapped. 'Didn't you find him?'

'Afraid not, Mr. Drew. The car was deserted. We're making a search, of course, but this is as far as we've got up to now.'

'All right, keep on searching,' Drew

directed. 'And thanks. That's all.'

The police sergeant left without further words and Drew chewed hard on his cigar, scowling at the closed door.

'Just what do you think Brant's up to?' J. K. Darnhome demanded, getting up and going across to the decanter to refill his glass with whisky.

Drew turned to him deliberately. 'Brant isn't up to anything, J.K. He wouldn't dare; I know too much about him. The answer to this one is that Brant has either been kidnapped or else is injured or dead. Nothing else would cause him to disobey my orders. And I don't like it!'

'But there isn't anybody who can know what sort of — er — work Brant does for you,' de Brock objected.

'That's the part I don't like. It looks as if somebody is on to me, and the only person I can imagine in that role is Quinton's daughter.' Drew pulled at his cigar pensively then with a jerk of his heavy shoulders returned to the armchair. 'Well, I'm pretty sure I can count Brant out from now on, which is a pity. I'll have to get another man, that's all, and it won't be too easy . . . However, we are here to discuss business, not Brant. And if you've finished drinking my whisky, J.K., perhaps you'll come over here and join us.'

Darnhome drained his glass, refilled it and brought it over, poising it on the arm of his chair.

'Well?' Drew asked him. 'Are things going on all right?'

'In the main, yes. But to make mass production of the bomb is going to take me a few months — getting the necessary metals, I mean. They'll have to be imported and that means using every possible subterfuge to avoid running foul of the atomic power defense regulations.'

'I realize that,' Drew said. 'But there's no fear but what things will work out all right finally, is there?'

'No fear whatever!' Darnhome took a few sips of the whisky and set the glass down again. 'What makes it doubly slow — and difficult — is not being able to come out into the open. Preserving a secret between the three of us isn't so easy.'

'Four,' Drew corrected. 'You're forgetting Valant, my head man. He's keeping it to himself, too — and he will. He knows what will happen to him as well as to us if anything at all suspicious gets out.'

De Brock smiled cynically. 'Not much chance of that!'

'You think not?' Drew regarded him and then gave a grim smile. 'It may shake your complacency to know that Scotland Yard is straining every nerve to get some sort of line on we three — and it was Jaline, the daughter of Quinton, who started it. Assisted by my own personal secretary.'

'Scotland Yard?' De Brock gave a start. 'Hmm — have to be extra careful. Thanks for the warning, Drew.'

'For me,' J.K. said, squinting into his half-empty glass, 'something now ties up. I read in the paper today that your secretary was the victim of a car accident yesterday afternoon. I couldn't quite understand it at the time. Let's see now. It just gave her name. Janet Kayne. That was she, wasn't it?'

'Correct.'

'And Brant finished the job, I suppose?' Darnhome emptied the whisky glass.

'It had to be done, J.K. I couldn't let her walk about with as much information as she possessed — not only in connection with Quinton, but other things that she might have recalled to mind. On the other hand, she deserved all she got for betraying my confidence and teaming up with Jaline Quinton closely enough to tell so much to Scotland Yard. She mentioned your name and de Brock's. So, it seemed expedient to be rid of her.'

'And since then somebody has disposed of Brant very neatly,' de Brock said, musing. 'Have you no ideas on it at all, Drew?'

'None — and I'm not worrying my head about it until I have to. I've a new secretary starting to work for me tomorrow, and I've double-checked her. She's safe enough.'

'She'd better be,' de Brock said uncomfortably. 'There's an aura of mystery over this business which I don't half like.'

There was silence for a moment as they all three drew at their cigars and considered the leaping flames of the fire.

'Anyway,' Drew said at last, 'to get back to matters. What about your arrangements, Brock? You fixed up?'

'I'm pretty much in the same spot as J.K. here. In fact a worse one, if possible. I'm head of Atomics, don't forget, and the law is keener on my organization than anything. It's going to be about six months before I can sort things out so as we can get the necessary explosives for the Quinton bombs — '

'They're Super-Bombs from now on,' Drew interrupted, 'Quinton's name must never be mentioned in connection with them any further!' He stopped and pursed his lips. 'Six months, eh? Well, better to take that long and avoid slips than give the law a chance to get at us. Anyway, I daresay it will take me that long to polish off all the formalities with the international dealing. I've started the wheels moving, though. There'll be results before long.'

He got to his feet and threw the stub of his cigar into the fire.

'Both of you must never forget that

we're playing with brimstone until we get this thing properly organized — and I can't repeat too often that the secret is ours alone. We're going in direct opposition to the law and we stand to get life imprisonment if we're caught — especially if our activities in removing certain factions can be proven. There must be no mistakes! None!'

★ ★ ★

Joyce Sutton arrived in the Drew Building right on time the following morning and from the moment Drew smiled on her as she entered the office she knew the job was hers. The remainder of the day she spent in accommodating herself to her new occupation, and within three more days she had settled down to her work quite efficiently.

There was plenty she questioned inwardly but she was wise enough not to mention it. Drew, too, seemed entirely satisfied. Then on the Saturday morning, as she was about to depart after taking dictation, he detained her.

'By the way, Miss Sutton . . . '

She turned enquiringly and waited. Drew was pondering something, standing beside his desk and rubbing his jaw.

'Yes, Mr. Drew?'

'I'm just wondering — Do you happen to know anybody whom you could recommend to be my private chauffeur? I've advertised and interviewed several men but none of them has proved suitable. My former chauffeur has — er — retired from that sort of work and I'm in something of a fix.'

Joyce considered for a moment or two and then gave a faint smile.

'Well, sir, I do know one man — yes, but whether he'd ever consider such a position I can't say. He's rather highly connected socially, I understand. Lives in Mayfair and drives a car of his own.'

Drew grimaced. 'Mayfair, eh? Mmm! I agree with you it's hardly the district whence a chauffeur should hail. Still, maybe I can make it worth his while. Who is he?'

'His name is Peter Maxton. As a matter of fact you've seen him already.'

'I have? When?'

'He was in the outer office the other day when I applied for this position. Don't you remember telling him that you never employed male secretaries?'

Drew looked surprised. 'Oh, *that* chap! The one with the matinee-idol face! Well, now — This begins to look a bit more promising. He was looking for a job as secretary; maybe he'll take on something else in the same organization. Are you — engaged to him, Miss Sutton?' Drew's brows lowered suspiciously.

Joyce shook her blonde head.

'Remembering your warning that you don't like your personal secretary to be involved with anybody, I'm not. I just happen to know him as a friend. And for my own part I think he might be interested in your offer.'

'Good! Is he on the telephone?'

'Yes. Mayfair seven six four one.'

'Thank you, Miss Sutton. I'll see what I can do.'

The girl nodded and left the office. Drew thought for a while, then picked up the telephone.

'Get me Mayfair seven six four one — a Mr. Maxton.'

Once connected it did not take Drew long to make his business clear and in fifteen minutes he had Larry Clark sitting at the opposite side of the big desk, smiling, completely bland innocence on his good-looking face.

'That you're interested in this proposition of mine, Mr. Maxton, is obvious by your coming here,' Drew remarked.

'Of course I'm interested, sir! Having high social connections but precious little cash isn't much use to me. Besides, I'm the kind of chap who likes to get about.'

'Yes; so I understand from Miss Sutton. You are here entirely on her recommendation. Naturally you drive?'

'Any kind of car you care to mention.'

'Mine's a Chrysler — that is the one I use most.'

'Suits me,' Larry said, nodding.

'And you're well set up ... Drew contemplated him. 'Strong, eh?'

'Strong enough. Middle-weight champion of my college. But how does that apply, sir?'

'Oh, just that I might have a heavy job or two for you to do when we get to know each other better.' Drew gave a grim smile. 'For the time being you'll limit yourself to driving. What references can you offer?'

'Only the references of friends. I never worked for anybody in my life before. New experience for me, sir. Still, you can make any enquiries you may wish. Suppose I write down the particulars?'

Drew nodded and pushed a sheet of paper across the desk. He sat watching as Larry wrote steadily. Altogether he spent several minutes on the job, then he nodded to himself as if satisfied.

'There you are, sir — everything. When would you like me to come back for your answer?'

'You don't have to. I'll ring you up either way the moment I've made my decision.'

Larry nodded and got to his feet. 'I'll be around waiting for it, sir — and thanks.'

'There's one thing I would warn you against, Maxton . . . ' Drew looked at him steadily. 'You and Miss Sutton are great friends. I'm not raising any objections about that, providing it does not go any further. Understand? I don't care for my employees to become entangled with one another. Should anything in the nature of an engagement take place between Miss Sutton and you you'll both lose your employment here instantly. I'm simply warning you. That clear?'

'Perfectly clear,' Larry acknowledged calmly. 'Neither of us would be such fools as to throw a good thing away. Good morning, sir.'

''Morning.'

As he passed into the corridor from the reception office Larry beheld Joyce Sutton peeping round the edge of her door, waiting for him.

'Any luck?' she asked him eagerly, as he hurried towards her.

'I don't know yet — but it's more than possible. Depends if he likes my background, and I can't think why he shouldn't. But unless he rings me up before evening I shan't be able to keep that date tonight. I've got to wait at home for him to say something. You do understand, don't you?'

She smiled and nodded. 'Of course, Peter. Anyway we've been out most nights this week.'

'There's only one thing I don't like — this rigid ban on engagements among his employees. I'd rather hoped — '

'We've our livings to earn, Peter. Let's be sensible.'

He smiled. 'Glad you look at it that way. Well, I must be going. Wouldn't do for us to be seen talking together like this before I've even got the job. I'll keep you in touch with whatever happens.'

He patted her hand gently and walked on down the corridor to the elevator. Smiling rather tightly to himself he jumped into his open roadster and drove back to his Mayfair flat. Without pause he went across to the telephone and dialed on the private wire to Scotland Yard.

'Hello, Chief . . . Larry here.'

'Glad to hear from you again, Larry,' Poole's unhurried voice responded. 'How are you getting on?'

'Beautifully. I stand every chance of

becoming Drew's new chauffeur.'

'You do!' A trace of eager excitement came into Poole's voice. 'Now that's really worth hearing! How in the world did you manage it? Answer the ad. he's been putting in the paper?'

'No. I didn't think I stood much chance that way. That girl I told you about — Joyce Sutton — arranged it, quite unconsciously. I've clung to her so's I could have a line on what old man Drew is doing and now she goes and pitchforks me into the job of chauffeur, which makes it easier still.'

'And Drew has no suspicions?'

'Not as far as I can tell. No reason why he should have. He must know we're working on him, but this thing's happened so naturally and I look so genuine I don't think there's anything to fear. He's checking up on the references and particulars I gave him but they'll stand up to it all right.'

'Splendid!'

'Any news yet concerning the missing Brant, or Quinton's daughter?'

'Nothing on Jaline Quinton, no. She

hasn't returned to the hotel and all our efforts at trying to trace her have failed so far. We're still on the job and other police departments up and down the country have been informed. As for Brant, I have the idea — or rather Divisional Inspector Grayham has — that Brant was thrown down a disused mine shaft near the spot where Drew's car was found. There's a quagmire at the bottom of the shaft and anybody falling into it head first would undoubtedly sink — and vanish. Falling horizontally you'd just be able to reach firm ground with feet and fingers. There are plenty of footprints but they don't amount to much as far as evidence is concerned. The mine's being examined now.'

'Uh-huh,' Larry acknowledged. 'Come to think of it, Chief, Drew wasn't lacking in nerve when he told the police he'd lost his car and chauffeur. You'd have thought he'd have stayed as far away from the police as possible.'

'Why should he? He knows we've no proof of anything he may have done, and he *had* to report his vanished car because it would have been found anyway and it would have looked even queerer if he hadn't mentioned it. Naturally, the local police are taking care of it, but since everything Drew does interests us I've got full reports of what's going on.'

'All right. Well, that's about all, Chief — except to tell you that I'm not making any personal visits to the Yard from now on, and naturally none of you chaps must be seen coming here. I'll make all communications over this private wire. The rest is up to Drew and whether he engages me or not.'

'There's one thing,' Poole said, his voice dry.

'Yes?'

'How much do you care for this girl Joyce Sutton?'

'Well, er — ' Larry grinned to himself. 'Quite a lot, as a matter of fact — enough not to want her to get mixed up in anything messy. Why?'

'Watch out for yourself, that's all. You can't afford one slip, Larry, and the last person I'd trust is a girl whom I hardly know who wangles you into the position of the boss's chauffeur. She *may* be up to something: never can tell.'

'That makes two of us, then,' Larry said calmly. 'Leave it to me, Chief: I can look after myself.'

He hung up, gave a brief troubled frown, then lit a cigarette.

7

That Emerson Drew accepted him as his new chauffeur, with hints that he might eventually become his strong-arm man, Larry took as a matter of course. He could hardly see how things could have worked out otherwise — and at first, for a month in fact, he did little but act purely as chauffeur, always smiling, prompt, and generally efficient — but he had ample time to get his bearings, lay plans of his own, draw rough designs in his notebook of the various positions of the offices, research laboratories, and general layout of the Drew Building.

One point that interested him quite a deal was that Joyce Sutton's office adjoined that of Drew's, and that there was a fair-sized mirror embedded in the wall of Drew's office — which wall was also that of Joyce's. He even measured the exact size of the mirror when he had a few seconds alone in which to do it.

Another interesting point was that there was a private hotel directly opposite to the Drew Building. Thus far Larry got and revealed nothing to anybody except Inspector Poole, and this over the private wire. Several times, either at the office or at the Drew residence, Larry came across de Brock and Darnhome and made notes of the fact — but apparently most of the private conferences took place in the locked confines of Drew's office, sound-proofed at such times and once, even, with shutters drawn over the windows.

Even in his off time Larry did not have much chance to escape from the business on hand. It was spent mainly with Joyce, and he tried by every means he could devise to trick the girl into some unwary admission — uselessly. She came through with flying colors every time.

There seemed no reason to suppose but what she was entirely genuine, with no axe of her own to grind, or on behalf of Drew. Larry's inner suspicion that perhaps she was a 'plant' of Drew's gradually died a natural death. After six weeks of close contact with her, and his position of confidential chauffeur more or less assured, he began to move out into the open — carefully.

He chose a time when Joyce and he had an evening together to make his first moves. They had been to a show and were having supper in the Golden Grill when Larry played his opening gambit.

'Joyce, if you knew a man to be a murderer and a swindler; if you knew he had two cohorts as black as himself, and you had the chance of bringing the law down on top of him, what would you do?'

The girl looked at him in surprise and lowered her coffee cup.

'Now what in the world led up to this, Peter?'

'You'll see,' he answered quietly. 'Just answer the question — if you can.'

She shrugged. 'Doesn't take much answering, does it? Naturally I'd help — if I had the opportunity.'

Larry considered his cigarette for a moment, then his eyes studied her.

'You have,' he said.

She made a puzzled gesture and he went on, 'I'm taking an awful chance on you, Joyce, and if I'm wrong it may cost me not only my job but my life! But if I'm right it will help to land three of the most cold-blooded criminals in the country behind bars. That I tell you this is the measure of the faith I have in you.'

'Peter . . .' Joyce's voice was deliberate. 'What in the world are you talking about?'

'I must correct a mistake just here, Joyce — I'm not Peter; I'm Larry. Larry Clark.' He felt inside his coat. 'Here — read this. I only carry it about when I'm not on duty with Drew. Otherwise it's safely locked away . . .'

He handed over a well-polished leather wallet and the girl opened it slowly, frowning over the warrant card staring up at her:

Criminal investigation Department, Metropolitan Police, Special Branch. Name: Lawrence Clark. Rank: Detective-Inspector first-class. Height 6ft. 2in. Weight 14 stone. Hair, black. Eyes, dark blue. No distinguishing marks.

'Detective! You?' The girl stared at him. 'Well, of all the — I just can't believe it!'

'Well it's true, whether you can or not. My job is to get the goods on Drew — and de Brock and Darnhome too if I can. I think I know how I can do it, too, but I'll need your help. You are in the offices all the time and I'm not. That is why I tried to get the job as secretary, and failed. I was just trying to cook up something else when you landed me as chauffeur. You'll never know how good a turn you did me, and the Yard. Now you can see what I meant when I said I was taking an awful chance on you.'

The girl handed him back the warrant card slowly. There was an expression on her face that he found difficult to fathom. It was not exactly surprise now; it was more like a suppressed amusement. Then gradually it faded as a new thought evidently took possession of her.

'Does this mean that you've kept so close beside me all because of your — work? Has *that* been the reason for your attentiveness?'

'Partly, yes; partly, no.' Larry looked at her entreatingly. 'I didn't know I would ever meet you as I did: it was sheer chance. Everything else apart, I'm immensely fond of you and I've done my best to show it. I even warned you of the danger of becoming Drew's secretary because I didn't want anything to happen to you. I can't make you believe that, of course, but I would honestly rather be with you for yourself alone than for business reasons.'

Through a long interval Joyce mused, pulling at her underlip gently, then at last she smiled and patted Larry's hand.

'All right, Larry, I believe you. I'll help you — but it's liable to put me out of a job. How then?'

'I'll see you don't suffer — believe me. For the moment, all I want from you is information. You know the mirror in the wall of Drew's office — the one on the other side of your wall?'

'Why, yes.' Joyce's look of wonder returned. 'What about it, anyway?'

'What is on the wall of *your* office which corresponds in position to the mirror?'

'Why — er — there's a large framed picture of the Drew Works in its early days. You find such things in lots of offices. Then there are other pictures of the Drew organization in various stages of growth — '

'Never mind those,' Larry interrupted, musing. 'So a picture covers the wall behind the mirror. Good!'

'Does it matter?' the girl asked.

'It matters a good deal, as you'll discover later. Believe it or not, my next important move is going to be to quite accidentally break that mirror in Drew's office. *Then* you'll see why!'

★ ★ ★

'Are you crazy?' Inspector Poole asked over the private wire early next morning when Larry rang him up. 'Taking that woman into your confidence? And since when has the police department asked private individuals to do their work for them?'

'The police are glad of all the help they can get, Chief, so don't hand me that one! The girl's quite safe: I've tested her in every possible way and she didn't give herself away once. I've worked things out and I want you to get me an X-ray mirror made to the following specification — two feet by one, with beveled edges. Later on I'll give you the tip to send in a man to fix it — in Drew's office. I'll need a sixteen millimetre camera too. Tell the recording men to stand by for a call. I might need them any time.'

There was something resembling a chuckle from the other end of the wire.

'Sounds as though you intend to do this thing in quite a big way, Larry.'

'I do,' he retorted. 'I want all the evidence we can get in sound-photography — and I'll get it! For the moment that's all, Chief. I've got to be moving. I've to pick Drew up in the car at quarter to ten. 'Bye for now.'

Larry rang off, picked up his chauffeur's cap and left the flat. Right on the minute he picked up the financier from his residence and drove him at a sedate pace into town. Then as he held the car's rear door open for him to alight he spoke — half hesitatingly.

'Excuse me, Mr. Drew but — I think

there is something you might like to know.'

'Well?' Drew looked at him uncompromisingly.

'You mentioned when I took over this job that, in time, you might need me for — er — heavier work. In the time I've been working for you I've found out, from one or other of the staff, that that kind of work means bodyguard stuff — strong-arm business.'

'So?'

'I wondered if you thought I'd been long enough in employment to trust me yet, sir? I'm willing — if you are. I've been practicing up on my shooting, too.'

Drew eyed him steadily. 'Apparently you take your work quite seriously, Maxton.'

'I want to be a success at my job, sir, if that's what you mean. For instance, a bodyguard can't afford to be a novice at shooting. I'd like to give you a little demonstration if I may — in the building, of course, where we won't attract attention.'

'Got a gun with you?'

'In my coat, sir — a thirty-two. It's a revolver I've had for a long time. Licensed, of course. I bought it for personal reasons in the days when I had far more money than I have now.'

Drew reflected briefly and then jerked his head towards the building.

'All right, I'll see what you can do. The sooner you start to fall into my ways, the better. Come on.'

Larry nodded in suppressed satisfaction and followed the broad stocky figure up the steps and through the entrance hallway to the elevator. When they had reached the private office Drew took off his hat and coat and strolled over to the desk.

'Okay, show me what you can do. And don't be too long over it; I've a lot of work to get through.'

Larry felt inside his livery and tugged the revolver from the shoulder-holster he was wearing. Then he looked about him, went over to the small table in the corner near the wall-mirror; rolled a tiny piece of paper into a ball and placed it on the table top.

'This should prove it, sir,' he said, sighting — then he pulled the trigger and the revolver exploded deafeningly.

The paper remained where it was but there was a violent splintering from the wall as the embedded mirror fell outwards in javelin shards. Drew looked at it, at the oak paneling of the wall behind it, then tightened his lips.

'Your aim isn't exactly perfect, Maxton,' he commented sourly. 'If my life depended on your being an accurate shot at that moment I rather think I'd be stretched out cold by now.'

Larry looked at the revolver stupidly, then at the shattered mirror — then both Drew and he glanced up towards the door as it was suddenly opened and Joyce Sutton looked into the office anxiously. Her eyes went to the shattered mirror, then turned to look back at Larry, and finally Drew.

'It's all right, Miss Sutton — though I don't wonder that you are startled,' Drew said. 'Just a demonstration of how not to fire a revolver, that's all. You can return to your work.'

'Yes, sir,' she assented, frowned, and then retreated.

'For the time being,' Drew went on heavily, as Larry put the revolver back in its holster, 'you can forget being my bodyguard and stick to your driving. Keep on practicing if you like, and in a year or two you may be a passably good shot. Until then keep your damned gun out of my way!'

'Yes, sir,' Larry agreed morosely. 'I — I could have sworn I was far better than that. I'll pay for the mirror, of course. It was my fault.'

'Glad you realize it. Get somebody right away to come and fix it — and the less the bill the better for you. I don't want any delay, remember: I use that mirror for shaving when I'm detained in here.'

'Yes, sir, I'll see to it. When will you want the car again?'

'I'm not sure. Go and find a man to do this job and then wait in the staff room downstairs. I'll ring when I want you.'

'Right, sir.'

Still looking crestfallen Larry departed,

but in the corridor he grinned to himself and patted the bulge where the revolver was holstered. As he had anticipated, Joyce was looking at him round the edge of her outer office door.

'It worked,' he murmured. 'Don't be surprised if the fellow who repairs the mirror burrows right through the oak paneling. I'll explain later.'

'I should hope so!' the girl replied, astonished.

Larry went on his way downstairs to the Chrysler, then he threaded through the back streets until he came to his flat. He wasted no time in getting on the wire to Inspector Poole.

'Chief? Things went better than I'd expected. I'm ready for that X-ray mirror to be fitted. Who are you thinking of getting on the job?'

'Wilford. He looks like a natural-born British workman — or don't I have to tell you?'

'You don't. Here's the angle. Tell him that the wall where the mirror is — or was, since I've smashed it — is oak paneling. There may be soundproof fibre as well; I don't know. In any case he must make a clear two-inch orifice through the wall into the adjoining office. That's where Joyce Sutton works.'

'Oh-ho! So *that's* why you teamed up with her?'

'Partly, and also because I like the way she smiles. However, fortunately for us there is a big picture covering the wall in Joyce's office where Wilford will make the hole. It has to be large enough to take a sixteen-millimetre camera lens and allow room for vertical and lateral movement. Get the idea?'

'Naturally,' Poole assented. 'Wilford will camouflage his actions well enough to prevent Drew knowing what he's doing. And how about the movie camera? What do you propose?'

'I'm handing it over to Joyce. She is the only one who has the necessary facilities for observing what's going on in Drew's office. I certainly can't because I'm not allowed to go in there, except with Drew occasionally. Joyce doesn't know yet what the X-ray mirror is for, but she will.'

'Okay,' Poole agreed. 'I'll have the

camera and film chargers delivered to your flat during the morning. Calvert will be there to pick them up, won't he?'

'Nothing surer.'

'And what about the recording unit you mentioned?'

'There's an hotel directly opposite the Drew Building. Get some of the recording boys in a room there, at the front. I'll tell you later what I'm aiming at.'

'Right,' Poole agreed; then he added dubiously, 'I still say I'd feel a darned sight happier if you didn't trust this woman so much. If you've made a mistake I'll never know what becomes of you.'

'On the other hand, if I'm right — as I am, I'm sure — you'll have all the necessary evidence for picking up Drew, de Brock and Darnhome. A time is bound to come when they'll assemble together in that office to discuss their plans, and when they do — well, things won't be as private as they think. If that should fail I'll have to think of a way to get into Drew's home, but I'm trying this first because the difficulties are not so great.'

Larry replaced the telephone, left instructions with Calvert, his bogus manservant, and then left the flat. He returned as quickly as possible to the Drew Building and then headed for the staff room as he had been instructed.

He phoned up to Drew and told him that a man would be coming to fix the mirror, to which he merely received a grunted response. There, for the moment anyway, his worries ended. He pushed his peaked cap up on his forehead, lit a cigarette, and then began to indulge in small talk with the weary-faced janitor until the big man should have need of him again.

Several times during the day he took Drew on various trips, but he never had the chance to observe what was going on in Drew's office. When, however, he felt reasonably sure that Drew would be occupied in his office for about an hour, Larry risked coming upstairs and poked his head round the edge of Joyce's outer door.

'Eight tonight at the Golden Grill,' he said softly. 'And bring an empty attaché case with you . . . '

Then before the girl could utter a word he had disappeared, to occupy himself as best he could until Drew should need him again. To his relief the only call was to take Drew home, and by six o'clock he was off duty.

He garaged the Chrysler, had tea in a city café, then went on to his flat to change, shave, and get out his own car. When he left he was in possession of the 16mm. camera, inside an attaché case. He put it on the seat beside him in the car and drove off into the traffic, arriving outside the Golden Grill right on time — 8-00 p.m. To his satisfaction Joyce was already there, pacing up and down slowly outside the restaurant, a small suitcase gripped in her hand.

'Good!' Larry told her, as he clambered out with his own attaché case and joined her. 'This makes my evening complete! Come along inside.'

Her bespectacled eyes appeared to look at him in vague wonder, then she went ahead of him across the restaurant to their usual table in the corner. She settled her suitcase next to her. Larry put his attaché case on the chair beside him, pulled off his hat, then sat down to regard her in silent amusement.

'All right, all right — everything's as clear as mud,' she said, spreading her hands. 'And I'll take coffee,' she added, as the waiter hovered.

'Coffee for both of us,' Larry finished, and waited until it had arrived before he spoke again. Then with a grin he asked, 'Well, how did the workman get on with the mirror?'

'Frankly, it was a good job you warned me what to expect! He came right through the paneling with a drill, clean through paneling and sound-proofing fibre. There's a two-inch wide hole now behind that picture of Drew's first factory. But just before he left the workman gave me a circular piece of wooden paneling exactly the right size to fit the hole. He told me to keep it there and clean up all traces of sawdust under the picture. I did that — and I doubt if anybody could even tell there *is* a hole, except by close examination.'

'And the picture covers it, anyway,' Larry added. 'Good! That sounds like nice work on the part of Wilford — the workman, that is. And the mirror? How does it look?'

'Just like the one you smashed — screwed deep into the paneling by all four corners. Naturally Mr. Drew never noticed what was going on. I suppose he assumed that the drilling was in order to screw down the four corners of the mirror.'

'It was — except for the addition of the little tunnel in the center.'

Joyce stirred her coffee. 'I still don't know how you managed to smash it with a revolver — the other mirror, I mean. What did you do?'

Briefly Larry told her and she gave an impish smile, then it slowly faded and she frowned.

'I just don't understand that new mirror,' she said. 'When I look at it in Drew's office it looks like any other mirror — reflects everything perfectly. Yet when I peeped through the hole in my office wall, after taking out the wooden plug, I could see right into Drew's office as though only a sheet of clear glass was in the way! What sort of a stunt is it, anyway? Black magic?'

'No. Not even gray. Simply polarized glass.'

'What in the world's that?'

'It's a scientific invention, used pretty extensively both here and in America — particularly by the F.B.I. — for the purpose of viewing while remaining unviewable. It reflects light-waves in one direction only. A person looking into the mirror on the mirror side sees only the normal reflection. A person *behind* it sees clean through it. Some private cars owned by Royalty and celebrities are fitted with it — in glass and not mirror form. They can see outside, but nobody can see into the car because the windows appear black. X-ray glass, as it is popularly called, has the advantage of being completely warpless and therefore perfect for photography.'

Joyce sighed and shook her blonde head. 'Well, it still smells like ye old witch doctor to me.'

'From now on, Joyce, the serious part

begins . . . ' Larry laid a hand on hers and looked at her earnestly. 'First, you had better take a peep at this.'

He hauled his attaché case forward, glanced about the deserted restaurant, then opened the case and brought the flat 16mm. camera into view. Carefully he laid it in the girl's lap and, hidden by the bulk of the table, she examined the instrument circumspectly.

'It's ready loaded,' Larry explained. 'Do you know how to work it?'

'Uh-huh,' she assented, studying it. 'Just the same as a nine-point-five camera — only better. I do a lot of amateur movie work with a little camera of my own.'

'That's perfect!' Larry enthused. 'All right, then, put it away in your suitcase and take it with you to the office tomorrow morning. You can do that?'

'Easily enough: I take a small case to the office every day in any event — a towel, some sandwiches, and odds and ends. I'll fit this camera in it and nobody will notice I'm bringing anything more than usual.'

'That's co-operation plus,' Larry said,

grinning. 'Keep it beside you in the office and when you know that Drew is talking with Darnhome and de Brock — or only one of those men for that matter — lock both your office doors and photograph everything they do, simply by holding the camera to the hole in the wall, which is in a direct line with the desk in Drew's office. You understand?'

'Yes,' she assented. 'Will the film hold out?'

'It ought to. The footage indicator will show you. If it starts to run out you'll find two spare charges fitted inside.'

'All right — but what will all this prove?'

'With sound added and synchronized to it, it will prove a good deal. I'm coming to that part. Your job will simply be to photograph everything you think worthwhile in Drew's office. Now put the camera away and I'll explain further.'

Larry waited until she put the camera down gently into the suitcase, then he went on:

'From today, a group of sound-recording technicians from the Yard are going to be stationed on twenty-four hours duty in the hotel directly opposite the Drew Building. They'll have field-glasses trained on the window of your office. If you stand at that window for a moment and press your handkerchief to your face they will know that it means they are to start recording. Follow?'

'You mean I do that when I'm about to photograph something?'

'Correct — and they will record the sound, but only you can do the photography.'

'But — how will they record sound? Drew's office isn't wired, is it?

'It will be after tonight, and in such a way that he will never suspect it. The microphone will be behind the speaker cone of his interphone and the wires will be woven into the heavy cable wire that normally leads to the interphone. He'll never notice the added wire even if he looks for it. The wire will then be connected to the main telephone cable leading outside and our men will get a line on it leading into the hotel. They will get all ordinary conversation on that line as well, of course, but they'll also get every word uttered in Drew's office, relevant or otherwise. Understand?'

'Yes — but . . . ' Joyce frowned for a moment. 'Why don't they listen all the time and save me signaling? Not that I mind, of course — '

'They *will* listen all the time, in relays,' Larry explained patiently, 'but they'll only start *recording* when you signal.'

Joyce nodded. 'Ah, now I get it! And there's something else that I'm wondering about. Will the light be good enough in Drew's office to get a good photograph? Suppose he holds a conference in the late evening or something with only a desk light on?'

'It's panchromatic film. Every detail will be seen on it.'

'And if his most important meetings take place when I've gone home?'

Larry shrugged. 'That we have to chance. I'm hoping he'll keep you on hand in case of reference to some file or other.'

'Y'know . . . ' Joyce turned her blonde head slowly. 'I can't help wondering why you trust me with such a vital — assignment.'

'Simply because I've got to, Joyce; there's no other way. In this particular instance you have the supreme advantage, and neither I nor the Yard are likely to overlook the fact.'

She looked at him steadily for a moment and he could not be quite sure whether there wasn't a spark of humor kindling in the depths of her lens-masked eyes. Then once more she was intensely serious.

'Getting into Drew's private office won't be the simple job that you seem to think, Larry. He has a special lock on the door and only his key will open it.'

'I know, and the same applies to the interconnecting door between your office and his, doesn't it?'

Joyce nodded soberly. 'Afraid so. I can't open that door until he arrives in the morning. I've no key for it, and anyway it's a special one.'

'But there's nothing special about the window catches,' Larry said, smiling. 'I've made sure of that during the few times I've been in his office. I've also inspected the building from the outside and there are toe and finger holds down from the roof to that window. That's the way I intend to get in.'

'But — but you can't!' the girl gasped. 'If you slip it's a two hundred foot drop to the street!'

'But I shan't slip,' Larry assured her calmly. 'I've climbed worse facades than that on the Drew Building many a time, believe me — and I'm fortunate in that there's a back fire escape leading to the roof.'

'And what about the equipment and tools you'll need?'

'Pliers, torch, screwdriver, flat disk microphone and a coil of wire. They're all in the car at the moment, but when I climb down the building I'll be able to carry them easily enough in my pockets. And,' Larry added, getting to his feet, 'the sooner I get started the better. I know the old man's staying at home tonight. He's got a bridge party or something. I can do all I want to do in an hour.'

Joyce gave him an anxious look.

'Can't I help you in some way? Stand

guard or something?'

'You'll be taking risks enough as it is, Joyce, with that camera,' he answered, patting her hand. 'This is my worry alone. I'll be okay; you'll see.' He smiled. 'We'll meet again in the morning, and when you get anything with that camera — granting I don't see you in the meantime — put it in your case and take it home in the ordinary way in the evening. I'll fix up a date with you somehow.'

Larry put on his hat, nodded, and went off across the restaurant, paying the bill as he went out. Joyce sat looking after him and for a moment that strange, half-smile played about her lips.

8

Larry Clark succeeded in his efforts for the simple reason that nobody had any reason to suspect him. He entered Drew's private office about 8-30 and by twenty to ten he was back again on the roof, his task completed.

During the period he had only had one anxious moment and that had been when the night watchman, making his rounds, had stopped outside the office door with his torch, hesitated, and then gone on. Nor had he returned, and as silently as he had climbed it Larry descended the main external fire escape and then vanished into the dark of the myriad alleyways to the spot where he had left his car.

As he had expected, when he rang up the Yard from his flat, Inspector Poole had left for home — so he waited until next morning before setting off to work in the usual way.

'Up to you, Chief,' he said, when the

preliminaries over the wire were disposed of. 'Get the boys into the hotel and have them stand by with a hitch on to the main line wire crossing the hotel. They'll get all they want.'

'They're already in,' Poole said. 'You tipped me off to that yesterday.'

'Good! And Joyce Sutton knows exactly what to do.'

'Sure she'll do it?

'Certain! She's in this to the hilt, and enjoying it.'

'Which is something I just can't understand,' Poole sighed. 'She knows she is literally going with her life in her hands and yet she does it. Must be some motive, or I don't know women.'

'Does anybody?' Larry asked dryly; then he hurried on, 'I suppose there's no sign of Jaline Quinton having returned?'

'No. Nor have we recovered the body of Brant or found out what happened to Rajek Quinton. We've taken over the Quinton luggage from the hotel, though, and we're holding it until we can get a definite line to work on. Not much doubt any more but what Brant was thrown down the mineshaft, but to recover his body from the quagmire — if that's where it is — is impossible. Anyway, we'll see how much *you* can find out.'

'*And* Joyce Sutton,' Larry added calmly. ''Bye, Chief.'

He put the telephone down and left for his day's work in the usual way. He could tell from Drew's manner that there were no suspicions in his mind, and drove him to the Drew Building along the same streets in the same period of time . . .

So there began the game of watching and waiting with Larry inwardly fuming at the lack of results and Poole calm but grimly patient.

A week — two weeks — four weeks went by, and nothing happened. In relays the recording men kept incessant watch from the hotel opposite. Joyce reported to Larry that so far nothing unusual had happened within Drew's office. There were times when Larry debated the advisability of trying to penetrate Drew's home, decided the risk was not worth it, and so went on waiting.

Another month passed and it was

mid-winter. It was actually early summer before something happened, nearly five months later, and then Larry did not know of it until he met Joyce in the Golden Grill in the evening, an appointment they had kept most working nights in order to remain in touch.

Larry knew the moment he saw the girl's expression when they met outside the restaurant that she was excited.

'It worked!' she breathed, grasping his arm. 'Darnhome and de Brock came this morning — there was a long conference. They discussed the blueprint and the model bomb — '

'The model bomb! You photographed it?'

'I photographed everything, including all three men as they studied the model each in turn. I don't know exactly what they said, but they *must* have discussed Quinton's invention. I suppose the recording men would look after that — '

'Your case!' Larry interrupted, noting she only had her handbag with her. 'Where is it? The camera?'

'I didn't wait. Those three men met this

morning, so at lunchtime I took a chance and went with the camera to Scotland Yard. I felt safer with it out of the way and I knew they'd want to develop the film as quickly as possible. I saw Inspector Poole, and I — '

'Oh, you did! How did you know whom to ask for?'

'I didn't,' the girl replied, shrugging. 'I gave my name and said I wanted to see the man who was working with Larry Clark — and they took me to Inspector Poole.'

'Hmmm!' Larry looked at her admiringly. 'You know your way about all right, don't you? Well, then what happened?

'Mr. Poole thanked me quite a deal and said that when I saw you — I told him I'd be meeting you this evening, of course — we were to go over to the Yard and join him. He said it would be worth the risk now we'd got things this far — '

'Then what are we waiting for?' Larry demanded. 'Here, hop in the car.'

He opened the side door of his roadster and the girl clambered in. Quickly he settled at the steering wheel and started the car forward.

'You're quite sure you weren't followed to the Yard this morning?' he asked, as he manoeuvred through the traffic.

'Well, I can't exactly be *sure*, but I don't think I was. Nobody suspects anything.'

'You took the hell of a risk.'

'Yes . . . ' Her voice sounded half amused. 'I suppose I did.'

'You've been wonderfully co-operative,' Larry said presently, but he was frowning to himself. 'There have been lots of times when I've wondered why. After all, I had no right to ask you to do anything. You could quite reasonably have refused — and yet you didn't. Was there any particular reason why you helped me?'

She nodded. 'Oh, yes! A very particular one!'

'What?' Larry glanced at her briefly then back at the traffic.

'Just here isn't the time to tell you — and anyway a driver should keep his attention on the wheel.'

Larry grinned to himself and said no

more. In another seven minutes they were at New Scotland Yard and found Chief Inspector Poole and Detective-Sergeant Jones waiting for them.

"Evening, Chief,' Larry acknowledged, smiling. 'I take it that I don't need to introduce Miss Sutton?'

'No, I've had the pleasure. How are you, Miss Sutton?'

'Full of excitement, I'm afraid, Mr. Poole. What sort of a cine-camerawoman did I turn out to be?'

'First class! If you ever tire of secretarial work let me know and maybe I can find a job for you — '

'I hate interrupting this charming conversation,' Larry put in, 'but did Joyce get what we've been waiting for? Can we nail Drew, de Brock and Darnhome?'

'I think so,' Poole assented grimly. 'I've been through the sound recording but I've yet to see the film. Anyway, everything is ready in the projection theater so come along and let's see how things are. The photographic department compliments you, Miss Sutton, on your handling of the camera. Very steady. The

153

sound boys have matched up the recording in synch. with the film.'

He opened the rear door of his office and the others followed him down the corridor outside to a door marked *Projection Room 1*. They entered and sat down in the gloom, Larry and the girl together and Poole and Sergeant Jones on either side of them.

Poole picked up the telephone to the projection-box.

'All right, Terry, let 'er go.'

A dim whiteness of screen came into sudden life at the end of the long room and a loudspeaker hissed with power. Unfolding in the dark was the scene the girl had photographed through the wall of her office that morning. Larry saw her straining forward to catch the words that up to now had been barred to her.

'Well, gentlemen,' Drew said, placing his fleshy hands palm down on the desk, 'it's taken us some little time to get the details fixed up, but I take it we are now ready? I know I am, and have been for some time.'

'As far as I am concerned,' Darnhome

said, setting the inevitable glass of whisky down on the desk, 'there'll be an uninterrupted flow of metals to your various organizations from now on, Drew. I've managed, and nobody knows what the metal is for. Nor will they. I remembered what you said. Only you, de Brock and Valant know, outside of myself, the secret of the Quinton bomb . . . '

'Lovely!' Larry breathed, rubbing his hands. 'He couldn't have done it better!'

'I told you we'd dropped that name!' Drew snapped at him. 'It's the Super-Bomb, and for God's sake don't forget it! One hint of the name of Quinton and hell-fire will descend on us — ' He turned to look at the atomic industrialist. 'How about you, de Brock? Everything fixed?'

De Brock nodded. 'Atomic explosive in unlimited quantity can reach you whenever you want it. That being so, suppose you tell us how *you've* fared?'

'I don't have to go into details,' Drew replied coldly. 'I'm paying for most of this, don't forget, and for that reason I can reserve my own secrets. I've made the necessary contacts and that is all that

matters. There's one thing I *do* know — '
Drew picked up the model bomb and
contemplated it admiringly — 'and that is
that Rajek Quinton was definitely a
genius. Almost makes me feel sorry I had
to eliminate him.'

'*If* you did,' de Brock sighed, taking the
bomb from Drew's unresisting fingers
and inspecting it.

'If I did!' Drew glared at him. 'What
the devil do you mean by that?'

'I was just thinking about that ex-chauffeur
of yours, Brant, whom nobody has ever
heard of or seen since the day he
vanished. To say the least of it, it was
an odd business and I've never felt
thoroughly easy in my mind since.'

'What's that got to do with Quinton?'
Drew demanded. 'To the best of
my knowledge Quinton was completely
eliminated — and Brant wouldn't make a
mistake over that because he wouldn't
dare . . . '

'The best of us make mistakes, Drew,'
de Brock corrected, handing the model
bomb to Darnhome as he reached for it.

'The fact remains that somebody had

an almighty powerful grudge against Brant and dealt with him most effectively. Since Brant hadn't polished anybody off for months until it came to Quinton's turn it seems to suggest to me that perhaps Quinton escaped and repaid Brant in his own coin.'

Drew reflected, his lips tight, then he shook his cropped head.

'I don't believe it!' he declared stubbornly. 'There's some other reason . . .'

'Funny, too, how the daughter dropped out of sight,' Darnhome commented, pondering as he put the model bomb on the desk. 'Ever hear anything more about her?'

'Not a thing. Not that I care what has happened. We have this business completely under control now and nothing anybody can do can alter it.'

There was a pause for a moment — then suddenly the film cut off in mid-action and the sound faded. The lights came up in the projection theater. 'There's more, of course,' Poole said, stirring in his seat, 'but it isn't of much use to us. We've got all we need in what we've seen. I'm taking out warrants for the arrest of Drew, de Brock and J. K. Darnhome. If we can't prove a great deal on the murder issue to begin with we can at least arrest them for contravention of the atomic power regulations. The rest will follow in natural sequence.'

'Right enough,' Larry agreed. 'And what happens to me now? Do I step down?'

Poole shook his head.

'It wouldn't do, Larry. Drew would suspect something if you suddenly failed to turn up. It is essential that none of those three men has the least idea of what is intended. And it will be towards tomorrow afternoon before I'm ready to pick them up, anyway. In the meantime carry on as usual until you get fresh orders.'

'Okay,' Larry agreed. 'You'll pick up Valant, too, of course?'

'Certainly. Darnhome mentioned him in his conversation as one of the sharers of the secret.' Poole got to his feet and looked at Joyce as she rose too. 'As for you, Miss Sutton, I doubt if we can ever be grateful enough for what you've done — particularly as it looks as though your employment with Drew may be in jeopardy. If that should happen come and see me: maybe I'll be able to help you out.'

Joyce smiled. 'Thanks, Mr. Poole — I'll remember that. Though I can't see that the removal of Drew should stop the whole organization. However, I'll look after myself.'

'That, Larry said, regarding her, 'is what I don't understand about you. I never knew a woman to take dangerous work so casually. Of course, there is *one* way in which you could assure your future — '

'I know,' she agreed, calmly. 'But maybe I don't want it that way — yet.'

Poole scratched his chin and regarded the pair of them.

'Seems to me that the best thing you can both do is stop talking in riddles and leave here as unobtrusively as you can. Get back to your 'action stations.' Things will happen tomorrow, quickly enough!'

* * *

When Larry had driven Drew to the office as usual the following morning he retired to the staff room until a call should come, and to his surprise he received it within five minutes. His surprise deepened and verged on alarm when he entered the private office to behold Joyce Sutton there also. Yet surely it wasn't possible that Drew could have discovered anything? It had all been too carefully planned for that.

Drew said nothing for a moment or two. He was reading a telegram and frowning; then he suddenly aimed his steely gray eyes at Larry.

'Fix the car up, Maxton. We're going to Yorkshire. I expect we'll be back by tonight. In fact I'll have to be. I've work to do.'

'Yorkshire sir?' Larry repeated, his astonishment quite genuine.

'You heard what I said!' Drew snapped. 'Miss Sutton will be coming too. I'll probably need a secretary. Mr. Valant will be with us also.'

160

'Yes, sir,' Larry assented, gave Joyce a helpless glance, and then left the office.

'All right,' Drew said briefly to the girl. 'Get whatever things you need for the trip, in the way of secretarial stuff, and join me in the entrance hall in five minutes.'

'Yes, Mr. Drew.'

She went through the interconnecting doorway and Drew frowned at the telegram again. It was brief — and certainly puzzling —

Have located Quinton. Definitely alive. Meet me immediately at Bedlington House, Tifley, Yorkshire. Bring Valant with you — Douglas Brant.

Drew rubbed the end of his nose pensively and then snatched up the telephone and dialed on the private line to the de Brock organization. There was no answer, which meant only one thing: de Brock was absent from his post. Only he knew the secret of answering on that particular line. Grimly Drew tried the atomic king's home and the manservant responded.

'No, Mr. Drew, I'm sorry. Mr. de Brock

left home early this morning on business. He did not intimate where he was going.'

'Hmmm . . . ' Drew tightened his lips. 'All right.'

He tried again — this time J. K. Darnhome. The result was the same. No answer at his firm and at his home a servant explained he had left early for an important conference out of town.

'Then Brant must have wired them as well,' Drew muttered, stuffing the telegram in his pocket. 'Funny — Something I don't quite like about it yet I don't see how I dare ignore it. If Quinton *is* alive — '

He glanced up as the outer door opened. Larry was there, cap in hand.

'The car's ready, sir. Miss Sutton is in it, waiting.'

'All right. I'll be down in a moment.'

'Yes, sir.'

Larry retreated and returned downstairs and to the car parked at the kerb. With a baffled look he settled at the steering wheel and regarded Joyce beside him. Her heavily-lensed eyes turned to him.

'What do you make of this lot, Joyce?'

he murmured. 'What's bitten the old man?'

She shrugged. 'No idea. Pretty obvious that telegram has something to do with it, but I've no idea what's in it. It came about five minutes before Drew arrived and I took it.'

'Yorkshire . . . ' Larry mused. 'That covers a pretty big area. And why Yorkshire, I wonder? I don't like it — It's going to upset the Chief's plans for making an arrest and I've had no chance to let him know what's happened.'

'Drew did say we'd be back by tonight,' Joyce reminded him. 'I hope so, anyway. I've no clothes, night attire, or anything with me.'

'Do you suppose,' Larry asked slowly, 'that he knows something about you and me and is, to put it melodramatically, taking us for a ride?'

Joyce frowned and pondered over the possibility, then both of them glanced up as Drew came down the building steps, followed closely by the lean-faced, lanky Valant, chief scientist. They got into the back of the car and Drew spoke briefly.

'Get going, Maxton. You won't need any directions until you get within the boundaries of Yorkshire. Until then head in that direction as fast as you can make it. Never mind speed limits: I'll attend to that.'

'Yes, sir,' Larry assented, and began the journey.

He drove by way of St. Albans, Bedford and Kettering, stopping in Leicester for lunch. It was only the briefest of halts, Larry and Joyce dining at one table and Drew and the cadaverous Valant at a distant one by the window — then again they were on their way, traveling with smooth swiftness through Nottinghamshire, and so at last into Yorkshire. By early afternoon they had reached York. Here, with the shadow of York Minster looming in the distance Drew ordered a halt.

'Ever hear of Tifley, Maxton?' he asked curtly.

'Tifley?' Larry frowned and reflected. 'No, sir — can't say that I have. Is that where we're going?'

'Yes. Hop out to one of these shops and

see if they can direct you.'

Larry nodded and descended to the street, walked along until he came to a tobacconist-cum newsagent-cum post office. Without hesitation he went across to the enclosed telephone box inside and shut himself in. After what seemed an exasperating waste of time he was speaking to Inspector Poole in London.

'Haven't a minute to lose, Chief,' he said quickly. 'I'm taking a risk doing this. I'm in Yorkshire, heading with Joyce, Drew and Valant to a spot called Tifley. Don't know any more than that. Figure it out for yourself. 'Bye.'

He came out of the box and went over to the man behind the counter.

'Ever hear of a place called Tifley?' Larry enquired.

'Tifley? Tifley? Why, yes! It's between Northallerton and Kirby Moorside; about fifty miles from here due north-east. It's a pretty quiet sort of place — nearly a hamlet — right on the moors. Fairly hard to get at.'

'There's a road though, for a car?

'Sort of,' the newsagent said.

'Thanks.' Larry nodded and strode out of the shop. Drew looked at him sourly as he climbed back into the car.

'Took you long enough to find out, didn't it? Well, where *is* Tifley?'

'Fifty miles north east. I think I can find it all right.'

'There's to be no thinking about it, Maxton; you've got to! Once we get to Tifley start asking for Bedlington House.'

Larry nodded, pondered to himself, and drove forward again, the girl sitting tight-lipped at his side.

The scene changed gradually as the car sped onwards. Once they had crossed the river Rye in the shadow of the Hambleton Hills the undulation of the land altered. Instead they were passing along hard secondary roads with the endless gauntness of the Yorkshire moors on either side of them — faintly hummocked, clothed in sere grass, and completely deserted. Even the sunshine failed to provide any modicum of cheerfulness.

'Nice place to live, anyway,' Drew growled — about the first audible statement he had made to Valant during the entire trip. 'More I see of it the less I like it.'

Larry drove on steadily at a good fifty miles an hour and the terrain changed but little — until at last in the distance the gray ridges of hills came into view.

They passed a signpost — Tifley — 5; Middlesbrough — 25. Larry put on more speed. So finally they swept into a small township couched in the depths of hills and plain and having somehow a similarity to a mid-Western American town of the gold rush era.

Larry drew the car slowly to a halt beside a stolid, weather-beaten rustic tramping along with a dog.

'Say — ever hear of Bedlington House about here?'

'Eh?' The rustic turned and came to the car's open window. 'Bedlington 'Ouse, y'say? Aye, I heered on it. Be about ten mile further yonder. Real old place an' all, pushed back among them 'ills y'can see from 'ere.'

'Right,' Larry said. 'Much obliged.'

Tifley dropped completely out of sight as the car glided further along the rough, ancient road. It wound and twisted through frowning hills and bare, somber plain alternately, then at length they rounded a bend in the road and Drew gave an exclamation.

'There, Maxton!' He was leaning forward intently, hands gripping the back of the front seat, peering through the windscreen. 'That old house to the right there, set well back from the road. That'll be it.' —

Larry nodded and his wonderment deepened. The house, as they came nearer, looked forbidding and dilapidated. It was perched several feet above road level and a drive ran up to it beyond open iron gates. Plane trees waving forlornly in the breeze, clustered thickly on either side of the drive as the car swept up to it and to a stop at the front door.

Drew sat for a moment appraising the scene. The house was large and rambling, yet its windows were so tightly curtained with some kind of dark material they revealed no hint of what was beyond: rather they reflected the scene outside. There was a square, porticoed entrance porch and three worn steps leading up to it . . . and silence. It was intense. Only the sound of the wind in the trees, and for surroundings the brooding, impersonal hills and here and there the flat, windy stretches of the Yorkshire moors.

9

Emerson Drew made a movement at last.

'Wait here,' he instructed. 'I'll find out where we can leave the car.'

He clambered out with Valant beside him and they stood looking about them. There was a big garage — or rather converted carriage house to the right of the house, its doors locked. Whether any car had been along this drive earlier was not revealed: the hard gravel carried no traces.

Finally Drew jerked his head to Valant and went to the front door to ring the bell.

'Nice sort of dump,' Larry observed, as the girl studied the house with him. 'Reminds me of something described by the Bronte sisters.'

'I definitely don't like it!' Joyce hugged herself and gave a little shiver. 'I'm actually feeling creepy. It's all so horribly lonely. If Drew wants me to go in there

I'm not complying — unless you come too!'

'I'll come; don't worry. Hello! Somebody does live here then, after all!'

The massive front door had opened and Drew was talking animatedly to a calm-faced manservant. Finally Drew came back down the steps.

'You two had better come inside,' he said, looking first at Larry and then at Joyce. 'The servant will take care of the car. He'll have to make room in the garage.'

'But if we're leaving this evening, sir, why can't it stay here?' Larry asked in wonder.

'I'm not sure yet that we *are* leaving this evening. Do as you're told, both of you, and come on.'

Larry gave the girl a glance and then scrambled out on to the driveway. Together they followed Drew up the steps and the three of them joined Valant in the hall. Larry's eyes strayed to the front door as it closed and for a moment a vague sense of shock stole over him. The edge of the door was not wood, but *steel*. It clicked into place softly, so completely indeed, it was hard to tell there was a door at all. It might have been part of the wall . . .

The manservant, small, pale-faced, amazingly impassive, turned and advanced.

'If I may have your things . . . '

Drew hesitated, then with a shrug pulled off his hat and coat and handed them over. Valant did likewise, and so did Joyce.

Larry studied the manservant fixedly as he handed over his chauffeur's cap.

'Dark in here, isn't it?' he asked abruptly.

It certainly was. A dim electric globe sunken in a heavy bowl was the only illumination. If there was a window opening to the daylight there was certainly no trace of it. Grimly, impressed by Larry's remark, the party studied the hall afresh.

It was square, old-fashioned, with a staircase at the far end. Against the walls stood armory, and upon the walls themselves brass plaques and shields. Near the staircase, perhaps six yards away in a corner, a statue of Eros stood on a pedestal.

'Damned dark,' Drew agreed, and aimed cold enquiry at the servant.

'The window has been blocked up, sir, pending repair,' the servant explained, unmoved.

'What about the other gentlemen?' Drew snapped. 'Are they here yet?' And Larry gave the girl a surprised glance.

'Yes, sir, they're here — waiting. If you will come this way.'

The servant led the way across the hall and threw open a door. Beyond was a wide, comfortably furnished room, but there was again a complete absence of daylight. Illumination came from an obviously new electrolier in the lofty ceiling. Somehow this complete change from daylight to artificiality was disturbing.

Dogged-faced, stolidly refusing to look bewildered, Drew marched into the big room and then came to a halt: J. K. Darnhome and de Brock were both there, standing beside the crackling fire . . . Joyce, Larry and Valant followed the financier in and gazed about them speculatively, particularly at the curtained windows.

'About time you got here, Drew,' J.K. said querulously.

'I got here as quickly as I could. I set off from London the moment I got this telegram.'

Drew pulled it from his pocket and the two other men produced their telegrams also.

'All alike,' Drew said. 'It's as I expected even though I don't understand it. They had to be answered, of course. This matter may be serious.'

'What baffles me,' de Brock said slowly, 'is where Brant is! He hasn't shown up yet.'

Drew gave him a bitter glance and nodded towards Larry and the girl as they stood listening.

'What of it?' de Brock asked cynically. 'If they don't know the facts now it's inevitable that they will before we leave here. Here, you two — read for yourselves . . . ' and he threw his own telegram on to the table.

Drew plunged his hands in his coat

pockets and stood watching. Larry read the telegram half aloud —

'Have located Quinton. Definitely alive. Meet me immediately at Bedlington House, Tifley, Yorkshire. Douglas Brant . . . '

'Well, where *is* Brant?' Drew demanded, wheeling round. 'Do we have to stand around here like kids at a guessing game? What's that damned moon-faced servant got to say for himself?'

'Nothing,' de Brock growled. 'He says we'll understand very shortly.'

'Oh, he does!' Drew compressed his lips and considered. 'Hmmm, come to think of it this may explain why Brant disappeared. He's been trailing Quinton — and to a cockeyed house like this, too, apparently . . . '

Drew stopped as the manservant appeared silently in the doorway.

'If you would care to see your rooms — Madam? Gentlemen?'

'Rooms!' Drew echoed. 'What should we want to do that for? We're not stopping here! Fetch Brant immediately and let's have an end to this tomfoolery!'

'I am afraid there is no Mr. Brant here,

sir,' the servant answered quietly.

J. K. Darnhome, a slender hip-flask half-way to his lips, lowered it and put the cap back on it mechanically.

'Not here!' He jerked up his head and stared. 'Then what — '

'Who,' de Brock asked deliberately, 'sent those telegrams and signed them as 'Brant'?'

The manservant gazed back at the atomic king steadily.

'I'm afraid I don't know, sir — but I have little doubt that everything will be made clear to you presently. In the meantime I am merely endeavoring to follow instructions.'

'Whose?' Drew barked.

The servant did not reply. Drew clenched his fists.

'All right, I'm leaving. Come on, Valant! You too, Miss Sutton — and you, Maxton.'

Larry, the girl, and Valant did not stir. They were too amazed to realize what Drew had said. Glaring at the servant Drew swept past him through the doorway and into the hall. After a moment or two Drew came striding back, a look of angry astonishment on his face. He stopped in front of the manservant and gripped the lapel of his coat fiercely.

'Look here, you, I'll not stand for having games played on me! I'm Emerson Drew, understand? Nobody does as they like with me! Get that front door open!'

'You mean — you can't open it yourself?' Valant asked blankly.

'No! It fits into the wall so tightly there's hardly a line to show where it is. No locks, no keyholes, no damned handle either as far as I can see . . . ' Drew swung round bitterly. 'Why leave everything to me? Didn't you look for yourselves? You two were here before me, anyway.'

'Only an hour before,' de Brock said. 'Anyway, we had no reason to look round: we thought you'd explain everything.'

'Well, I can't — and *you* start talking!' Drew shook the manservant savagely — but it was no use.

'I'm sorry, sir,' he said finally. 'I can only ask that you be shown your rooms.'

'Better do as he says, Drew,' Darnhome said uneasily. 'Going off the deep end isn't going to get us anywhere.'

Drew hesitated and then dropped his hands.

'All right!' His voice was harsh. 'Where are these rooms?'

'There is something I must make clear,' the manservant added. 'Rooms are prepared for you, Mr. Drew — and for Mr. Darnhome, Mr. Valant and Mr. de Brock. There has been ample time to arrange them to your taste, but in regard to you, madam, and you, sir — ' he looked at Joyce and then Larry — 'you were not expected. I hope you will forgive the slight evidences of haste that may be apparent.'

Neither Larry nor the girl said anything. The whole business seemed too utterly unbelievable — preposterous.

'I still don't understand what kind of jiggery-pokery is going on here,' Darnhome snapped. 'How *can* we stay here? We've no clothes, no night attire — '

'Forgive me, sir, but each room is supplied with whatever you may need — suits, pyjamas, razors, everything. The two rooms not so prepared are those of the young lady and gentleman here. Perhaps — you will be able to manage?'

'Apparently we'll have to,' Larry replied shortly.

The manservant looked vaguely relieved and motioned into the hall.

'If you will come this way then — '

The party followed him across the dimly lit expanse, past the faintly illuminated statue of Eros, and so up the stairs and to the long corridor at the summit. There appeared to be nothing particularly unusual about the bedrooms. They were well furnished and all that could be desired — but it was the pervading air of the unexpected that tried the nerves and brought frowns to every face.

'Dinner will be served in half an hour,' the manservant said finally and then went off quietly down the corridor.

The party remained where it was, watching him, ignoring the rooms they had been shown.

'I don't like this a bit,' Darnhome declared finally. 'Do you suppose we are prisoners?'

'In a perfectly ordinary house?' Drew snapped. 'Don't be an idiot!'

'If it were ordinary it would have a proper front door,' de Brock pointed out. 'And you say it hasn't. One thing is quite certain — Brant didn't send those telegrams. That leaves only one person for it, to my mind . . . Quinton!'

Drew set his jaw. 'Quinton died, I tell you! And Brant never made mistakes.'

'As I pointed out earlier, he could have done — for once. And if Quinton is at the back of this . . . '

They were silent, considering each other. But Drew's bulldog courage did not desert him.

'If it's Quinton we'll deal with him fast enough. A queer house and a mysterious build-up can't scare men of the world. Incidentally, how did you both come here — by car?'

The two men nodded.

'And chauffeurs,' Darnhome added. 'The cars are out in the road. If we don't appear soon our respective chauffeurs will get together and act for themselves.'

'I think you should know,' Drew said

slowly, 'that there were no signs of cars in the road when *I* arrived. Either your chauffeurs have driven off somewhere or else they have been taken care of!'

De Brock made an irritable gesture. 'Oh, to hell with this conjecture! Let's get tidied up and down to dinner. 'I'm feeling hungry . . . '

★　★　★

The dinner was perfect, magnificently cooked, plentiful, with spotless linen and shining cutlery. Unobtrusively, obviously well-trained, the servant glided about, attentive to every little want — yet with all the perfection the darkly-gathered mystery of the place hung over it. Each member of the party ate mostly in silence, working the problem out. Until at length the meal was over.

'You will find cigars in the lounge, gentlemen,' the manservant announced calmly. 'The first door across the hall.'

'Are you ordering us about?' Drew asked him bleakly.

'I am sorry if I conveyed that

181

impression, sir I merely felt that you would be more comfortable in there. In fact I imagine that you will find in there the answer to much that is puzzling you.'

'We will?' Darnhome asked abruptly, jumping up. 'Well, that's more like it!'

With a complete disregard for everything and everybody he hurried out of the room — and for that matter the others didn't dawdle behind him either. The lounge was brightly lit as on the occasion when they had all first met, the fire burning pleasantly.

Drew came to a stop, glaring round in expectation of seeing somebody. Then Larry hurried over to the big table in the center of the room and picked up an envelope.

'For you, Mr. Drew . . . '

He handed it over and the financier snatched it, tore the flap open and tugged out a sheet of quarto folded four times. He read, the others crowding round him. Breathing quickened at the words staring up in neat handwriting from the crisp paper:

Gentlemen: None of you will leave this house alive because it is my avowed intention to destroy you — one by one — as you tried to destroy me! Whatever you may do, wherever you may go in this house, you cannot escape me. I am judge and executioner, exacting a punishment that I deem to be just. You stole from me; you gave me hours of anguish, you have planned to disrupt the world with an invention which I intended only to be for defense, not offence. I am decided that you shall not succeed.

You are wondering about the full story — how I come to be alive, where my daughter is, how everything has been contrived? I would be a poor artist indeed if I painted the picture all at once. I shall reserve much of the truth until later on. Little by little you will learn everything, and when learned it will be useless to you! I trust you thoroughly enjoyed your last meal? I merely conformed to law in that your last meal should be without stint. For *the moment I leave you to think this over.*

Rajek Quinton.

'For God's sake!' Darnhome whispered, his eyes bulging as at last he looked up. 'The — the man is alive, and he's gone crazy! Drew, you damned fool, Brant must have slipped up somewhere after all. Quinton is here, in this house, watching us from somewhere!'

Drew jammed the letter in his pocket and set his jaw. No words escaped him as he weighed up the facts. De Brock rubbed his chin and then pulled out his cigarette case with a hand that was not entirely steady.

'There's something about that letter I'd like to point out,' he said.

'Well?' Drew glared at him.

'Quinton, if we assume that he wrote it in advance, did not expect Miss Sutton to be with us. He says 'Gentlemen.' In fact he probably didn't expect Maxton here to be present either. Remember the servant said that he and Miss Sutton were not — '

'Oh, shut up!' Drew interrupted savagely. 'I'm about sick of this schoolboy nonsense. Where's that servant — '

He strode to the lounge door, snatched it open and went out in to the hall. The others remained by the table glancing at each other, listening to Drew shouting and the noise of his fists banging doors. After a while he came back, looking both chastened and bewildered.

'He's gone!' he announced blankly. 'The table in the dining room hasn't been cleared. But *where* he's gone I'll be damned if I know. I can't find a door leading out of this place.'

'He wasn't a ghost, Mr. Drew,' Valant commented laconically. 'There must *be* a way out, and since Quinton is — or was — a scientist, he perhaps fixed the front door, the only visible outer door we've seen so far, on a scientific principle. Suppose I take a look at it and see what I can discover?'

He turned and headed from the room and the others followed him into the hall, to stand watching as he examined the panel-like front door carefully. As Drew

185

had remarked, it was hardly possible to discern the slit where wall and door edge were divided.

For a time Valant examined it minutely, going over every inch of it — then he gave a triumphant cry as a small protruding piece of metal at the extreme top of the door caught his attention. In an instant he had whisked a chair forward, stood on it, and seized the metal projection tightly. It pointed downwards, hollow at one end, rather like thin gas tubing and not more than half an inch of it showing.

The result of Valant's efforts was the exact opposite of what the party anticipated, however. The moment he grasped the projection there was a hint of peculiar bluish vapor from the pipe end, which gushed into Valant's enquiring, upturned features.

For perhaps five seconds he stood motionless, a look of deadly suffocating horror creeping over his face — then he pitched straight off the chair and crashed his length on the floor.

'What the devil — ' Drew gasped blankly; then hurtled himself forward, the others coming up behind him.

There was no doubt of one thing. Valant, chief scientist, was dead. His mouth gaped wide open, his face was bluish-white, the eyes rolled upwards.

'Gassed, or something,' de Brock said, struggling to make sense out of the tragedy. 'It came out of that pipe. It must have been planted there so somebody would grab it and — God, of all the filthy games to play! It's hitting in the dark!'

'So was the murder of Quinton,' Joyce remarked grimly — and the men looked at her for a moment in surprise. She seemed to have quite forgotten for the time being that she was a secretary.

'Quinton wasn't murdered, or he wouldn't be hiding in this house waiting to pounce,' Drew retorted, scowling at her. 'All right, so Valant's dead — lethal gas or something. We'll be wary next time. Quinton won't manage it twice.' He glanced about him and finally to the long oak seat by the far wall. 'Better put him there and cover him with his overcoat. Grab his ankles, Maxton. I'll take his shoulders.'

Grim-faced, Larry obeyed and the dead scientist was carried across the hall and laid down. Drew threw the man's overcoat over the body and then turned back to the group in the centre of the hall with Larry beside him. They exchanged glances as they beheld Darnhome studying another sheet of quarto, de Brock and the girl looking over his shoulders.

'Where'd you find that?' Drew demanded roughly.

'I noticed it on the floor when you picked up the body and carried it away,' the girl said, glancing up. 'It was rolled up flat and tight, like a little tube. It could have been ejected somehow from that pipe — '

Drew took it and began reading, Larry beside him:

Gentlemen: It is possible that by now you will have appreciated the fact that I am not making idle threats. Death in this instance was produced by inhalation of poison gas. You are also entitled to Explanation No.1:

I did not die as planned by Brant. He succeeded in disfiguring me for life, but he did not kill me. When I killed him I made sure of everything — even to his total disappearance in quagmire. I had £50,000 in notes in my hotel. I went and took them away from there — unrecognized — and used the money for buying and equipping this unique house. How unique it is you will shortly discover, and it has taken every penny I possessed to do it. I have had you watched, gentlemen — closely. You are not alone in having agents. I knew the best time to send those telegrams . . . and they were sent.

Rajek Quinton.

This time Drew was not ready with a fierce outburst. The second letter had shaken him badly though he struggled not to show it. He raised his eyes at length to meet the calm, accusing gaze of Joyce and the square face of Larry.

Then Darnhome made a little sound like a gulp and snatched the hipflask from his pocket. Before he could get it to his lips, however, Larry snatched it from him.

'That's enough whisky drinking,' he said curtly. 'We've quite a big sized problem on our hands, Mr. Darnhome, without you getting plastered for good measure . . .'

'Why, you damned insolent — ' Darnhome swallowed and glared. 'You seem to forget who you are — your position here!'

'On the contrary,' Larry retorted, jamming the flask in his own hip pocket, 'it's about time I made it clear to you just *who* I am. We're all in a spot in this house, and don't you forget it! I'm not your chauffeur, Drew — or anybody else's. I'm Larry Clark, Special Branch, Scotland Yard.'

Drew's self-control was such that his fists clenched and his thick neck went a shade redder at the back.

'I haven't my warrant card with me to prove it,' Larry added briefly, 'but it's true, whether you believe it or not. The Yard has the goods on you three men, in case you'd like to know.'

'And I suppose the Yard dug up this place to improve its chances of getting us?' Drew barked.

'No; that's the point. This house was never in our calculations and I'm as baffled as you are by what's going on — but I think this Quinton means what he says and that we've got to get out of here somehow — or die.'

'And walk right into Scotland Yard?' de Brock asked sourly. 'I'd sooner stay here.'

'And be murdered?' Larry enquired.

'We'll probably be that, anyway — or at least dead, with the law on top of us.'

Larry shrugged. 'Please yourselves, but I'm going to try and get out before Miss Sutton and myself get something that is perhaps intended for one or other of you men — '

'Just a minute, Maxton — Clark, or whatever your name is!' Drew plunged his hands in his coat pockets and regarded Larry fixedly. 'You say you're from Scotland Yard? You mean you faked everything to get into my employ?'

'Everything. And you swallowed the bait.'

The financier sighed and cocked his shaven head on one side reflectively.

'Yes, I'm afraid I did. I admire a neat job of deception, even if the Yard does put it over. Serves me right — ' His gray eyes strayed to Joyce standing quietly by. 'How do you fit into this, Miss Sutton?

'She doesn't,' Larry answered briefly; then he changed the conversation. 'Does it occur to you that we've been so busy concentrating on the door we've forgotten the windows?'

'Unless they're booby traps,' Darnhome pointed out

'Can but see. Come on.'

They looked about them and then cautiously approached the hall window that the servant had said was made up. Gently Larry pulled aside the curtains.

'By . . . heavens,' he breathed.

'Made up is right!' Drew snapped. 'That's solid steel plating!'

10

For a moment or two there was troubled silence, then Drew took a deep breath and glanced at his watch.

'Quarter to eight. Still be some daylight outside but none that we can see.'

Larry was examining the wall paneling carefully and presently he turned a grim face.

'This isn't oak paneling,' he announced. 'It only resembles it: actually it is steel, painted dark oak color.'

'This isn't just a house,' Darnhome said, with a trace of evident nervousness. 'It's — it's a steel box with Quinton watching us from somewhere, grinning like hell, I'll bet — *Quinton*!' He broke off, with a hysterical yell. 'Quinton, where are you? Come out and fight like a man!'

'There's one thing I'll tell you,' Larry said, as Darnhome's voice faded into the quiet of the house. 'When we stopped at that shop to ask the way to Tifley I rang up Scotland Yard and told Inspector Poole I was heading for Tifley. I couldn't tell him more then because I hadn't all the information. There's a chance he'll track us down, though whether he'll be able to get into this place any more than we can get out of it I don't know. It's pretty obvious Quinton spent most of his money converting this place into a prison — '

'Look!' Drew interrupted with a relieved chuckle. 'A telephone! Now perhaps we can get some action.'

He went to it where it stood on the table across the hall and whipped it up to his ear — then as complete deadness lay in the receiver his eyes dropped to a note neatly fitted along the top of the telephone cradle, visible now the instrument had been raised. It said, simply — *Dead, as you will be soon!*

'Damn!' Drew swore, and slammed the instrument back.

'That servant got out — so can we!' de Brock said abruptly. 'I'll get that front door open if I have to smash everything in the rotten house — '

He whirled up the chair on which Valant had stood and slammed it with hysterical, despairing violence into the door. He did it again, and yet again, whirling the chair round and over until it was splintered to pieces and he himself was quivering and drenched in perspiration. The door was adamant, its smooth surface hardly marked.

'The servant probably used a secret switch to open the door and get out,' Larry said. 'We might search forever trying to find it.'

'Then what the devil *do* we do?' Drew demanded. 'We can't wait around to be picked off, one by one. At least I'm not going to!'

'Then what are you going to do?' Larry asked him.

'I'll — I'll — ' Drew stopped, tugged out his cigar case savagely and jammed one of them in his mouth. 'I don't know yet,' he growled. 'Let's go back into the lounge and think it out somehow.'

They returned there solemnly and disposed themselves in various chairs, grim or thoughtful, according to temperament.

'What I don't understand,' de Brock said at last, 'is why Quinton doesn't *show* himself! You'd think he'd be here to enjoy the results of his villainy — and there's certainly been plenty of labor gone into the conversion of this house in the wilds.'

'A man with a mind like Quinton has probably no need to show himself,' Drew said. 'I've no doubt but what he's got this place fixed so that he can watch and hear us without being visible himself. Ten to one he's grinning right now as he looks at us and listens.'

'I don't call this a fair fight,' Darnhome grumbled.

'It was fair enough when you stole his invention,' Joyce commented — and as the men glared at her she added: 'Oh, I know all about it! I've no sympathy for any of you, and that's straight.'

'You're no longer my secretary,' Drew announced coldly.

'In our present predicament,' the girl said, 'that's the funniest statement I've ever heard.'

'I wonder,' Larry said, pondering, 'how this place is ventilated? The chimney's one way — but hardly enough — '

'Chimney!' Darnhome exclaimed, jumping up. 'Of course! Why didn't we think of it — '

He lunged across to the fireplace and began dragging out the burning coals quickly. One of them, brightly flaming, he picked up in the tongs and thrust it up the chimney for illumination. Then with a sigh he began heaping the coals back in the grate.

'Steel plating with small holes for the smoke to go through,' he announced bitterly.

'I hardly expected the chimney — or any of the chimneys — would be left open,' Larry remarked. 'But the fact remains there must be some way for stale air to get out and fresh to get in. I'm going to take a look round.'

'I'll come with you,' Joyce said, and getting up she followed him out of the room.

Together they went into the hall.

'You're saying what you think pretty freely, aren't you?' Larry asked her, in some curiosity.

'Why not? I don't believe they will ever get out of this house alive anyway, and I certainly don't intend to continue as a secretary in the Drew organization if *I* get out alive.'

'But I thought you said that you would?'

'It suited me then to say it; not any more — ' The girl's heavily-lensed eyes regarded Larry for a moment, then she hurried on, 'Anyway, I thought we were going to look for ventilators? Let's see what there is.'

She turned aside and both of them began a meticulous search of the walls. It was not long before they discovered minute holes drilled high up, utterly useless as forming the basis for an escape even though they admitted fresh air. They were also set at an angle so the daylight outside could not be seen.

'If only there were something somewhere in this place which would penetrate steel!' Larry sighed. 'Wonder if the kitchen has anything to offer?'

'Hardly likely that an electric drill will be left lying about, is it?' the girl asked dryly, but she followed him into the kitchen just the same.

The place could not have been barer. There was nothing that even resembled a tool, no trace of food, though water was in the taps, running slowly in a manner suggesting it was pumped from somewhere.

'I say,' the girl said presently, raising her head. 'Do you *hear* something?'

They were both quiet for a moment and presently detected quite clearly that which had arrested her attention. It was a deep, far away throbbing and seemed to be coming from an infinite distance beneath their feet.

'Power plant somewhere,' Larry decided. 'We've about as much chance of finding it as getting to the moon. Come to think of it, though, there must be a power plant of sorts or else we wouldn't have electric light in a deserted spot like this.'

'There might be batteries,' Joyce said surprisingly. 'And they wouldn't make a noise.'

'Mmmm . . . ' Larry looked at her, puzzled. 'You say things sometimes that make me wonder how much you really *do* know. You are a most informed secretary.'

'Ex-secretary,' she corrected. 'And if you don't mind I'll take these things off — they're making my head ache. I don't as a rule wear them beyond two hours at a time.'

She lifted the glasses from her nose and pinched finger and thumb to her eyes for a moment. Then she lowered her hand and sighed, folded the glasses up and put them in the case she took from her costume pocket.

'You look a darned sight better, without the things,' Larry said, studying her critically.

She smiled. Her blue eyes looked strained.

'Well, since we've found ventilation and heard a power plant we can't reach maybe we'd better go back and see what the three musketeers are doing . . . '

'Before we do — do you mind me saying I admire the way you are taking things? You didn't bat an eyelash when Valant died — pretty horribly too — and you're still not apparently much worried by the thought that if we are not murdered we may die of starvation.'

'Perhaps I seem callous because I'm sort of used to — the unexpected,' she answered vaguely. Then, brightening, 'Well, come on.'

Puzzling to himself Larry followed her out of the kitchen, across the hall and back into the lounge. The three tycoons were still there, Drew pulling at the stub of his cigar, Darnhome staring moodily into the re-made fire, and de Brock glancing uneasily about him as though he expected to be tapped on the shoulder at any moment.

'Well, what did you find?' Drew asked.

'There's ventilation — but it won't do us any good as far as escaping is concerned,' Larry answered. 'Another cheerful discovery is that there is no food . . .'

Drew did not seem to be listening. His eyes had fixed on the girl as she went thoughtfully to a chair.

'The more I see of you, Miss Sutton, the more I wonder if — ' Drew stopped and set his mouth tightly, following an unspoken thought.

For a moment the silence was complete, then Darnhome got to his feet impatiently.

'Give me that whisky flask!' he snapped to Larry, holding out his hand.

'Sorry.' Larry shook his head. 'I'm sticking to it. It's three-quarters full, and if you drink all of it you're liable to be so drunk we'll be handicapped trying to get you out of this if a chance to escape should come.'

'I won't drink it all! I only want a little of it . . .'

Larry did not answer. Darnhome met his steely eyes and muttered something to himself. What whisky he had had so far seemed to be having a slight effect. He was irritable, unsteady in his movements.

'Quinton or no Quinton, I'm going to bed!' he snapped, glaring round. 'Think I'm going to sit here and wait for something to happen? Not damned likely!'

He turned and went uncertainly from the lounge. The others heard his feet going across the metal-sheathed floor of the hall — then suddenly the brooding silences of the fantastic house were split by his hoarse scream and the distinct thump of his body.

Drew and de Brock were out of the room first with Larry and the girl close behind them. They found Darnhome sprawled at the foot of the staircase, gasping hard, lying on his face, a dagger buried to the hilt between his shoulder blades.

'F — fell. Downstairs . . . ' he whispered faintly, as Larry knelt beside him and turned him over. 'I — I got up a few steps and — and — '

'Who did it?' Drew shouted hoarsely. 'Who stabbed you, J.K.?

Darnhome looked at him fixedly, made a terrific effort to speak — then his head dropped limply to one side.

Quickly Larry took the Metal King's pulse. Life had ceased. He looked at the dagger, seized it, and whipped it out. It was a long-bladed affair with an ornate hilt, the blade somewhat weighted at the tip.

'What about fingerprints?' Drew asked.

'Why?' Larry asked him coldly. 'We've

got Quinton's letters for evidence if it comes to it — I'm not interested in fingerprints. All I want to know is who *did* this. Somebody stabbed Darnhome to death, either by throwing or actual hand action, and yet . . . '

Troubled, he gazed into the gloomy, dimly-lighted reaches of the hall. There just wasn't anywhere suitable for hiding — and the possibility of somebody in the armor was soon disposed of as, the same thought occurring to Joyce, she went over and took the helmet away. The suit was empty.

'Secret panel?' de Brock suggested huskily.

'I hardly think so.' Larry stood up slowly, frowning down at the body. 'Miss Sutton and I found the walls to be steel plating. That is, on the inside. Outside there's the ordinary brick — '

'Look!' Joyce interrupted, pointing. 'A note or something in the dagger hilt!'

Larry noticed her finger was indicating a tiny slip of paper jutting from the extreme end of the dagger hilt. He pulled it out and unwrapped a thin, tightly-folded quarto sheet. With grim eyes they all read:

> *Gentlemen: You will observe that I am still keeping my word — namely, the elimination of the three 'D's' — Drew, Darnhome and de Brock — and Valant, of course. You may take this present occurrence as guarantee that I shall fulfil all my promises.*
>
> *You are really entitled to Explanation No. 2 at this point, but perhaps it would be more subtle not to give it even yet! For instance, you must be wondering what has become of my daughter . . . You will learn — in time*
>
> *Rajek Quinton.*

Drew looked at Joyce Sutton pensively, then down at the sprawled body of Darnhome.

'We'll take him up to his room,' Larry said. 'Give me a hand, one of you.'

The fact that they had already carried a corpse across the hall, and were now carrying another up the staircase, was something that did not seem as horrible as it would have seemed ordinarily. Death in this weird, inexplicable house was something to be expected, and calmly met.

They left the dead Darnhome on the bed in his room — Larry and Drew — and then returned downstairs to find de Brock and the girl still in the hall, both of them looking about them for some explanation of how the knife attack had been made.

'I wonder,' Drew said, pondering, 'if we can get Quinton to show himself? We might do a deal even yet. I never knew a man who wouldn't listen when money talked, and he's admitted in one of his letters that he's spent up — '

He turned, cupping his hands round his mouth, and shouted. 'Hey, Quinton! If you are listening and are hidden somewhere — as I fully believe you are — how about listening to a proposition? Come out and call this whole thing off and I'll write you a check this minute for whatever amount you care to ask. It may walk me right into Scotland Yard, but I'll risk that too. You've been swindled and half-killed — I admit it — but you've had your own back. Come out, can't you?'

Silence — absolute, complete. Drew relaxed and mopped his forehead.

'I just don't get it,' he declared flatly. 'And what's more I don't intend to be scared any longer by all this hocus-pocus. I've a bed to sleep in and pyjamas provided, and I'm going to use both of 'em!'

He turned and went ponderously up the stairs. Larry, de Brock, and the girl, stood looking at each other.

'He's the biggest villain of the lot and yet he has the most courage,' Larry commented. 'I'll be hanged if I don't half admire him somehow.'

'Courage or otherwise he has the right idea,' de Brock said. 'I'm going, too . . . '

Larry stood eyeing the girl as de Brock went up the stairs. She took her eyes from the ascending figure at last and met Larry's level gaze.

'No reason why we shouldn't try and sleep, is there?' she asked. 'With one thing and another — to say nothing of the trip from London — I'm about tired out.'

'Why can't you behave like some girls I know and start to shudder?' Larry asked. 'Two dead men in the house and more death hanging like a cloud — and *you* suggest going to bed! What are you made of, Joyce — steel?'

'No, but I'm tired. No reason why I should miss sleep because two men who deserved it have been wiped out, is there? I'll just lie down as I am since . . . we were neither of us expected,' she finished quietly.

Larry shrugged and gave it up, followed her up the stairs and paused as she laid a hand on her bedroom doorknob.

'If anything happens or you notice anything queer don't forget to yell,' he said. 'I'm only next door, anyway.'

She nodded and he left her, went into his own room thoughtfully. For a moment or two he stood pondering, drawing a cigarette from his case. He lit it and sat down to think. The mystery of Darnhome's death lay heavy on his mind. With nobody anywhere near him he had met his deserts. Either the thing had been brilliantly planned by split-second timing — which seemed highly unlikely — or else the idea of a secret panel had to be entertained after all.

'And I don't like *that* either!' Larry muttered. 'When you talk about secret panels you're getting into hoary, hackneyed melodrama. I can't see a man like Quinton relying on a gag of that sort.'

He got up impatiently and paced the room. The absence of an ordinary window was deadening to him, producing a claustrophobic weight on his mind. He found himself wondering vaguely if Inspector Poole was perhaps somewhere outside trying to trace him. In that case there ought to be hammerings on the front door. Surely sound from outside would not be blocked? He remembered how Drew had rung the doorbell. Of course things had been very different then, and —

So he went on, asking himself questions and for the most part supplying the wrong answers. It was the sound of a throaty scream that finally brought his speculations to an abrupt end. There was no doubt about it. It had come from the next room — the one occupied by Marvin de Brock. Instantly he stubbed his cigarette into the ashtray and bolted for the door.

Drew had just appeared in the corridor outside, dressed only in trousers, shirt and slippers. His paunch was ludicrously obvious and there was startled wonder in his eyes.

'Did you hear something?' he demanded.

'From de Brock's room,' Larry answered briefly. 'Come on!'

He flung himself at the door of the atomic king's room and rattled the knob fiercely, banging with his other fist.

'De Brock! Hey, de Brock! You all right?'

There was no response and Larry gave Drew a grim look.

'Give me a hand,' 'he ordered briefly, and banged his broad shoulder against the door.

Between them they battered at it until

the lock snapped and they were impelled inwards. Halfway across the room they brought up sharply, staring at the bed. Marvin de Brock lay in it in a tangle of sheets, dressed in pyjamas, his hands at his throat. His eyes were staring horribly upwards in the light of the bedside lamp.

'Again!' Drew whispered, his forehead dewed.

Larry went forward slowly and stooped to look at the body more closely. Round de Brock's neck was a bluish line, obviously caused by intense constriction — yet there was nothing visible which might have explained itself as the cause.

'Strangled,' Larry said finally, biting his lip as utter perplexity came into his eyes. 'And done just as mysteriously and efficiently as the stabbing of Darnhome.'

'Perhaps,' Drew said absently, 'Quinton is a ghost . . . '

'Keep your feet on the ground, Drew,' Larry told him curtly. 'There's a logical, mundane explanation for these killings — but I'll be damned if I know what it is yet. Occurs to me there might be a note somewhere, too . . . '

He began to look about him and sure enough he came presently to a tube-like sheet of paper lying near the pillow. Picking it up he unfurled it slowly. Drew read with him:

To use the word 'Gentlemen' would now be incorrect. I fancy only one gentleman is left, and since that word is in itself an expression of respect I shall not use it. I would remark that trying to find me is futile — just as futile as trying to escape.

Rajek Quinton.

Drew scowled; then he turned as Joyce Sutton entered the room, fully dressed except for her costume coat. There was a questioning look on her face. Since neither man spoke she looked at the body on the bed and then turned away.

'Where have you been all this time?' Drew asked her harshly. 'What have you been up to?'

'Up to?' Her blue eyes regarded him coldly. She was still without her spectacles.

'I haven't been *up* to anything. I heard something like a scream, but since I was then half undressed I couldn't come right away. That satisfy you?'

'No, it doesn't,' Drew retorted. 'I'm more interested in the fact that you were several minutes behind Clark and me getting here. And I think that Quinton is in this house and that you know exactly where. I'm going to take a look while the trail is still hot.'

He went out of the room muttering to himself and Larry met the eyes of the girl from across the bed. She said nothing, however, and as usual seemed unperturbed by the proximity of the body.

'There's got to be *some* explanation for this,' Larry said finally, 'and I'm not going out of this room until I find it!'

He turned aside and began a meticulous examination of the furniture, under the bed, in the drawers — then suddenly Joyce arrested his attention with a little cry.

'Here! Look!'

Immediately he hurried to her side and

found her pointing to two tiny holes drilled in the steel-paneled wall. One was at the right-hand side of the bed-head and the other at the left. They were so neatly contrived, and so small, that their darkness against the general dullness of the paneling was hardly detectable.

11

'Definitely holes!' Joyce said, and finding a pin from some mystic region round the hip-band of her skirt she pushed it in the hole and pulled it out again. Going round the bed she did the same with the other hole; then she fell to thought.

'Listen, Larry, how's this for a theory? A cord — or maybe an extremely thin flexible wire, from hole to hole across the bed, was concealed in the bed-clothes in such a way that de Brock put his head in a noose without being aware of it. The moment he did so the wire tightened until he was strangled. Then the wire was released at one end and withdrawn through one of the holes.'

'Yes, it's possible,' Larry admitted, staring at her. 'And once again, you've got a surprisingly ingenious notion — for an ex-secretary. Assuming you are right that means that Quinton must be behind this wall somewhere.'

'Perhaps,' the girl answered.

'Seems to me to be the only angle of approach,' Larry went on. 'It would also help to explain the stabbing of Darnhome.'

'That's right. Unless . . . '

For some reason Joyce suddenly stopped, her eyes abstract, as though an idea had struck her. Then without a word of explanation she hurried from the room. Larry hesitated over following her, pausing as Drew made a reappearance. He was looking even more bewildered than when he had first departed.

Without a word he handed over a small paper slip — not of the usual quarto size. Larry read it under frowning brows:

There is a way out of this house. In the library you will find a concealed spring two feet from the floor, six feet from the made-up window. Depress it and a slide will go back to reveal a steel door. That is the way to freedom. I am a friend. I cannot say more now.

'Different writing to Quinton's,' Larry said, musing. 'And different paper, too.

Of course he could disguise his handwriting and use different paper, but — Where did you find this, anyway?'

'In the corridor outside — just lying there.' Drew passed the back of his hand over his sweating forehead. 'Don't ask me how it got there. I certainly didn't see it when I joined you in the corridor to break in here — and when I left you just now I went in the opposite direction, towards the stairs. It was there when I came back upstairs.'

Larry narrowed his eyes.

'Surely it isn't possible that Joyce . . . ' He looked up at Drew sharply. 'Looking at this thing squarely, Drew, she is the only one left now whose actions seem unaccountable. She *could* have left this note in the corridor before she came in here to join us.'

'Well, it's about *time* you got some sense!' Drew sneered. 'I've had my opinions about that young woman for some while. I believe she's Quinton's daughter!'

'You do?'

'I'm not dead sure, mind you. I saw the daughter before all this happened: in fact she held me up with a gun, but you know how it is sometimes when it comes to remembering faces. Anyway, this Sutton girl *could* be Jaline Quinton, particularly as the Quinton girl has dropped out of sight and Quinton himself in these demand notes of his doesn't seem anxious to tell what happened to her. If she *is* Jaline Quinton a lot of the mystery is explained away because it will mean that she is at the back of most of it. Incidentally — ' Drew looked about him '— I saw her dashing out of here. Where did she go?'

'Come to think of it, she didn't say.' Larry set his jaw. 'Come on — we've got to find her.'

They hurried out together — then when they reached the head the staircase they paused; looking below. They exchanged puzzled glances. Joyce was visible in the hall, but not very distinctly due to the dim illumination.

Her actions, to say the least of it, were unusual. She was creeping along with her back to the two men, absorbed in a study of the right-hand wall. Finally she seemed to be satisfied over something for she nodded to herself and, still walking backwards, came towards the staircase.

'What game's she got on?' Drew whispered. 'If she *isn't* connected with this business, I'm crazy!'

Larry made a silencing motion and they continued to watch, hidden by the massive post at the staircase top. Joyce's actions were now even stranger. She backed up four stairs from the bottom, gave a start, then started searching at her feet. Finally she picked up something that looked rather like a pellet of paper.

It was too much for Drew.

'What the hell ails you, girl?'

Joyce glanced up, startled for a moment. 'Suppose you come down and find out?' she suggested.

Drew set his jaw and came striding down the stairs, Larry behind him. The girl waited until they were on the same stair and then she pointed to the statue of Eros in the further shadows of the hall.

'I've discovered something,' she announced. 'Watch Eros's right arm — the one that's upraised.'

Drew and Larry did as she asked and then she threw her weight on the third step from the bottom of the staircase. The surprising thing was that Eros's right arm, held upwards in an impression of speed, flashed forward abruptly and then resumed its normal position as Joyce moved off the step.

'I put a pellet of paper in his hand to see where he aimed,' she explained. 'It hit me on the back of the head! Had it been a knife with a weighted blade, and had I been as tall as Darnhome, I'd have got it where he got it . . . in the back.'

Larry came down to the third step and tested it several times, watching Eros meanwhile.

'And we never noticed Eros much because of the gloom,' he murmured, thinking. He gave the girl an admiring glance. 'That's the best bit of deduction we've had in this business so far.'

'More accident than anything,' the girl said. 'When I came down here to look around after de Brock's death I happened to be looking at Eros as I came down the stairs. I saw him move and — well, there it is! I've been trying to trace some signs of wiring but I've been unlucky.'

'I don't believe a word of it,' Drew said grimly. 'I don't mean that I doubt Eros: that's the obvious explanation of Darnhome's death — but I don't believe *your* story. You knew all about it beforehand, same as you've known about everything. Now, to deflect suspicion, you're trying to look smart. Besides,' he went on, in a louder voice as the girl tried to interrupt him, 'how is it that the manservant took us all upstairs and we didn't get a knife thrown at us then?'

'Simply because the mechanism, whatever it is, was not set in action until the servant had left. From then on these stairs were a death trap and, as it happened, Darnhome was the first man to ascend them. Larry and I nearly did when we looked for a ventilator, but finding what we wanted downstairs here we had no need to go any further, and that undoubtedly saved our lives . . . The whole Eros business is flawlessly calculated — height, throw, action, everything. Any person of normal size going up the stairs

221

would have been bound to get the knife.'

Drew stared at her malignantly.

'You're sure you and Clark didn't go upstairs because *you* knew what would happen?' he demanded; then suddenly he seized the girl by the shoulders and shook her violently. 'Why don't you come out into the open, Miss Quinton, and admit your identity? Do you take us for fools? Do you think I haven't noticed how unconcerned you are about the deaths which have occurred? Of *course* you're not concerned! You're working for your father! He's dead, just as I said he was, and you've taken his place. Up to now you have worn glasses to prevent my realizing who you are. Now it no longer matters you've discarded them. You got into my employ through faked credentials and I relied on them enough, and the subtle differences between your face and that of Jaline Quinton, to think you really were a different person. Now I know what a damned fool I was.'

'Do you?' the girl asked quietly, pulling herself free.

'Read this,' he added, and pulled from

his trouser pocket the note he had picked up in the corridor. 'Only *you* could have put it there.'

Joyce took the note, read it, then handed it back.

'If a knife can be thrown automatically by Eros, a note could just as easily be ejected from somewhere into the corridor,' she said, when Drew had told her where he had found it. 'You might even have crossed a photo-electric beam or something which caused the note to be released. Certainly I wouldn't advise you to take any notice of this 'friend' who seems to be anxious to help. It is more likely a trap devised by Quinton who knows that by this time you'll be ready to take almost any chance to escape.'

Drew clenched his fists. 'Naturally *you* wouldn't advise me to escape! Why should you?'

'In that case,' the girl said coldly, 'you must doubt that I *did* put the note in the corridor?'

Drew glared but said no more. Joyce looked at Larry then back to Drew again.

'This isn't the best of places to talk,

gentlemen,' she said quietly. 'Come down into the lounge; I've something to tell you. Perhaps I should have told you earlier, but I wanted to keep quiet as long as possible.'

Puzzled but silent they followed her down the remaining steps and across the hall. She switched on the lights in the lounge and then settled herself in an armchair. Drew too sat down, a gross, heavy figure in his trousers and collarless shirt. Larry elected to stand, pulling a cigarette from his case.

'First of all,' the girl said, 'there's one thing you should get absolutely clear right now: I'm not Joyce Sutton, but — '

'Jaline Quinton!' Drew snapped. 'Made up!'

'No,' the girl said, shaking her head. 'I'm Virginia Crane, of the United States Bureau of Intelligence.'

Drew's expression slowly changed as he absorbed the astonishing fact and Larry pulled hard at his cigarette. Then the girl felt in the pocket of her blouse and handed across a small leather case. Larry opened it, nodded briefly, and handed it back. When Drew took it he stared as though he could not believe what he saw.

'Which accounts,' Larry said finally, 'for your lack of concern at the deaths around here, and your willingness to help me.'

'And for not behaving like some women you know and screaming the place down,' she added.

'I don't quite see what you have to do with the Quinton business,' Drew said, handing the case back. His voice had the subdued grimness of a man who knows he is in a corner.

'I'm not interested in Quinton. I wasn't assigned to that case at all. I was told to get the truth out of you about Travers, who as an American citizen became upon the report of death in mysterious circumstances, the concern of the Bureau of Intelligence.'

'Well, you'll get nothing out of me,' Drew declared, sitting back and folding his plump arms.

'All right, I'll say it for you. He met his death through your machinations, and Darnhome and de Brock were mixed up in it. I was sent to Britain to get what information I could and stumbled right into the Quinton affair.'

'Your credentials checked exactly when I engaged you,' Drew pointed out. 'It was only that fact that led me to employ you, otherwise you might have waited forever to muscle into my organization.'

The girl smiled faintly. 'If the post of secretary had not opened so conveniently, other ways would have been found. As for the credentials, they checked because they were intended to. A complete false trail was laid with the connivance of Scotland Yard, who are as anxious to get you as is my own department — '

'You mean Inspector Poole *knew* all the time!' Larry exclaimed.

'No, Larry . . . ' The girl looked at him. 'Only the Chief Commissioner and Assistant Commissioner. Nobody else. And even they had not a complete knowledge of what I was doing since I am not answerable to them.'

'And the spectacles?' Drew asked cynically. 'What was the idea of them?'

'Those? Oh, my explanation was almost

genuine in regard to them. I have been suffering from eye strain, but it's been a lot better in recent months.'

'And I thought you wore them to disguise the fact that you were Jaline Quinton, somehow changed,' Drew muttered. He rubbed a hand over his shaven head. 'I took the wrong road, and I admit it — but at least you didn't get anything.'

'In regard to Travers?' The girl reflected.

'No, I didn't. I might have done, only events moved so fast in the Quinton business I didn't get the chance.' She turned to Larry again. 'I realized though, that in helping you to get Drew in the hands of the law I'd help myself as well, because, accused of the Quinton crime, the rest would automatically follow. A general unraveling of unsavory truths would commence. That was why I helped you so willingly and took such risks.'

'How much did you help him?' Drew asked bitterly.

'To the extent of cine-photographing your interview with Darnhome and de Brock yesterday while Scotland Yard sound engineers recorded your voices.'

'It couldn't be done!' Drew declared flatly.

'It could, and it was,' Larry told him. 'The result is in the hands of Inspector Poole at this very moment. You remember how I smashed that mirror in your office?'

'Well?' the financier rasped.

Briefly Larry gave him the details. At the end of it Drew sat pondering, hands dangling between his knees, a tight smile on his lips.

'All right, you win,' he muttered. 'If one plays a dangerous game one must be prepared to lose. I thought it would happen one day, but not quite so subtly or by such scientific methods. You're surprised at the way I'm taking it?' He looked up and broke into a dry chuckle. 'You needn't be. I know I'm too much of a marked man by Quinton to ever reach Scotland Yard anyway. That being so I'm going to bed and to hell with the consequences!'

He got up, nodded briefly, and left the lounge. Larry's eyes strayed back to the girl as she sat thoughtfully in the chair.

'Now I know the reason for lots of things,' he murmured, coming over to her. 'I can see why you were so co-operative — and I'm sorry too.'

'Sorry?' She looked up in surprise. 'But why?'

'I'd rather hoped there'd be another reason for your helping me as you did.'

'Perhaps — there was.' She averted her face again. 'Even an official isn't always on official business. There is the human side — ' Suddenly she changed the subject. 'About this house, Larry: I've been thinking. That statue of Eros opens up a lot of possibilities, especially when one remembers the sound of a power unit buried somewhere under our feet.'

'Meaning?'

'Do you suppose that Quinton really *isn't* here at all? That everything that has happened — and may yet still happen — is really automatic?'

Larry gave a start, reflected, then snapped his fingers.

'Automatic! I do believe you've hit it! How much do you know about Quinton?'

'Nothing beyond what you've told me,

and that was pretty guarded.'

'The one thing about him I'm remembering is that in his own country he was a master-watchmaker, before he sold out and came to Britain. A master-watchmaker and a scientific inventor! What a combination! If he poured all his genius solely into devising a machine of vengeance he could do an awful lot of damage.'

Joyce — Virginia Crane — was nodding eagerly.

'You're right, Larry! The death of Valant was caused more or less by automatic means; we know that — and we know Darnhome died because of a similar mechanical set-up. That being so, there is no reason to suppose but what de Brock's strangulation was produced by similar means. Everything controlled from a power plant, which was probably set in action by the servant before he left, maybe by a time switch or something so it gave him time to get out.'

'What do you suppose happened to the cars owned by de Brock and Darnhome — and the chauffeurs?' Larry asked.

Virginia shrugged. 'How can I say?

Presumably the servant got rid of them somehow. It's possible we'd find the answer if we could get inside that garage.'

'The garage can wait. What we've got to do is to find where that power plant is and stop it before anything worse can happen.'

The girl nodded but she seemed to be thinking of something else.

'I'm sure Quinton isn't really here because of some of the things which have happened,' she said. 'The servant telling us we were not expected — that last note we got saying that there was only one left, whereas there are three if you and I are included. Then the fact that the word 'Gentlemen' has been used each time. Yes, the thing is working of its own accord, I'm sure, and the notes were planted beforehand. More or less they will be bound to sound consistent since only one person at a time would be likely to die in the order in which the notes have been found. More I think of this the more I realize Quinton has — or had — the mind of a genius, as well as that of a fiend.'

'Right enough,' Larry agreed soberly. 'Which leaves me wondering where he is now and what's become of his daughter.'

'He said we'd find that out — perhaps with the note that brings the end of Drew!'

'We've got to stop it somehow, Virginia,' Larry said. 'This sort of thing isn't justice; it's plain murder. I'm going to try and find that power plant.'

The girl got to her feet. 'Incidentally, Larry, what do you imagine that note means? The one Drew found in the corridor?'

'I think the same as you — that it's a trap, but if he is as desperate under his apparent calm as I think he is, Drew will start exploring. It's our job to stop it. Anyway, let's see where the power plant lies.'

They hurried out of the lounge together, and then in the hall they paused. Light was flooding from the open doorway of the library.

'Drew!' Larry said quickly. 'Although he did say he was going back to bed.'

It was Drew. They found him, still in

shirt and trousers, prowling along the wall near the window, pausing now and again and reading the note in his hand.

'Two feet from the floor . . . six feet from the window . . . Mmmm . . . '

'Not found it yet?' Larry enquired dryly.

The financier glanced up. He did not appear either surprised or angry.

'Not yet, but I will. If there's one chance of getting out of this death-trap I'm taking it. If you want to drag me to Scotland Yard afterwards you're welcome to try. But I've got to put an end to this damned suspense! Understand?'

'You're walking right into disaster, Drew,' Larry told him grimly, going across and clutching his arm. 'This place isn't being run by Quinton himself, but by clockwork or something — probably electric clockwork, too. Miss Crane and I have been working it out.'

'Clever of you,' Drew growled. 'Fact remains I'm not letting any chance slip — Hey!' he broke off in sudden eagerness. 'Eureka! We've got it!'

12

Beneath his roving, pressing fingers
something in the apparently flat paneled
wall had depressed slightly. In response,
on the opposite wall — leading away
from the hall — a steel door became
visible, perhaps six feet high and three
feet wide as a portion of the wall slid
aside to reveal it. Above the door was an
opaque sheet of gray glass about a foot
and a half square.

'It's it!' Drew cried, swinging round
with bright, eager eyes. 'Look! The note
says — 'a slide will go back, revealing a
steel door, which is the way to freedom!'
That's straight enough, isn't it?'

'I still don't like it,' Larry muttered,
studying the door from several feet away,
the girl at his side. 'Anyway, how do you
open it? I don't see any handle or lock.'

All of them appraised it critically, then
glanced at the table on one side of it,
upon which stood a solitary copper vase.

On the other side was an apparently normal bureau.

'Wish I could decide what sort of snare this is,' the girl said worriedly. 'Mr. Drew, I'm sure you oughtn't to — '

She stopped and Drew jerked his face upwards in surprise as the opaque glass screen over the door suddenly glowed white. The three backed away warily, ready for anything which might happen when to their astonishment a face appeared on the screen, so hideous, so burned, it made Virginia glance away in revulsion for a moment.

'Who the devil's that?' Drew jerked out.

'So you found the steel door?' a voice asked calmly, and there was something like a sinister chuckle.

Larry looked about him quickly but there was no sign of where the loud-speaker was fitted. In a house like this it might be anywhere, but from the direction of the sound it seemed to come from near the copper vase on the right-hand side of the door — perhaps even from inside it.

'I rather thought this way of escape would appeal to you,' the voice went on, and the lip actions of the hideous face matched exactly.

'Talkie film projection,' Virginia muttered, watching in fascination.

'You observe my face? This was done by a man named Douglas Brant. At the orders of Emerson Drew he threw nitric acid in my face and tried to kill me in a mine shaft. I escaped and threw him in the shaft instead, holding him down, *crushing* him down, until his body vanished forever and none could ever find him. Then I planned *your* destruction, contrived the suspense, the horror of never knowing when the sword of Damocles would drop! I will tell you now what happened to my daughter, my own Jaline, who tried so hard with a pitiful revolver to avenge what she thought was my death. She . . . died!' Cold, merciless venom came into the voice for a moment, and it paused. The image on the glass glared down as though it could see the three in the library.

'I — I never said anything about nitric

acid!' Drew shouted hoarsely, swinging on Larry and the girl. 'That must have been Brant's own idea. He always did carry things too far! I warned him about it many a time — '

'Yes, she died!' Quinton's shadow image resumed harshly. 'Quite by chance she saw me as I was returning to the hotel after having patched myself up after the injuries and burns I had received. She had a weak heart. I had not intended she should see me until I had arranged for a rubber mask to cover my mutilation. When she saw my face she collapsed in the street. I did not want a scene there and then and so supported her as a taxi came up. I got her into it.

'She recovered consciousness but I could tell she was gravely ill. I had the taxi take us right out of the city altogether and into the quietest part of the country I could think of — Tifley, the place we had decided upon as our possible retreat upon giving up city life. Just outside Tifley I found rooms and left her there for the time being with a quite motherly landlady who looked after her while I returned to

London — and incidentally dealt with Brant . . .

'I entered the hotel, went into my room, took away my money and left everything else. I did that for two reasons. I did not wish to draw attention to bags, and I wanted to be thought dead because of a scheme of vengeance that was maturing in my mind. If the law was tied for lack of proof I at least was not!'

Again the relentless voice paused. Drew did not comment this time but his face was wet with perspiration.

'When I got back to Tifley I knew my daughter was dying. She told me that Emerson Drew, Darnhome and de Brock — and Valant the head scientist — were the only men who knew my secret. That if they died the secret would die too. Then, even as the doctor attended her, Jaline died. Exertion, horror, nerve strain: they had all combined to kill her. She was buried outside Tifley, and on her grave I swore to destroy the four men directly responsible for her demise . . .

'I found this house, bought it cheap, converted it, made a friend of a man whom I knew I could trust — whom you have seen as the manservant — and then had various equipment and machinery sent, with which I did many things. When the time was ripe, telegrams were sent out from London to each of you four men. *I* sent the telegrams — or rather I *shall* send them since I am recording this before the event. Nor need you look for me in this house because I shall be giving myself up to Scotland Yard. My only hope is that each one of you is here, that the thought of my being alive will prove sufficiently alarming to bring you here . . . '

'You swine!' Drew breathed, clenching his fists. 'You dirty, murdering swine!'

'Naturally, I cannot know which of you is left to listen to me, but I can imagine that you are furious, furious enough to seize the nearest thing and hurl it at me — '

'By God, you're right!' Drew screamed, as he seized hold of the copper vase. 'I'll — '

He got no further. A mighty convulsive start shook him and his hand tightened round the vase like a claw. As if struck with a lightning bolt he crashed his length to the carpet with the vase still in his hand, a length of wire trailing from the vase's base and up through the center of the table on which it had been standing.

There was dead silence in the library. The voice had stopped and the image of Quinton's face had gone. The small loudspeaker that had been carrying the sound rolled out of the vase and stopped beside Drew's clenched hand.

Virginia took a step forward but Larry caught her arm.

'Electrocuted!' he said. 'Take it easy!'

'You — you mean — ' She stopped, staring at the financier's sprawled body.

'He was incited into doing that. Quinton certainly knows his way about when it comes to psychology. He planted that copper vase there, electrified it, and his hint to throw something worked! Drew died. Putting the loudspeaker in there also was a good idea. He knew the vase would be seized finally, if only to look for the loudspeaker.'

'And we know that we're not included

240

in the scheme,' Virginia said slowly. 'But that doesn't make getting out of here any simpler, does it?'

They fell silent for a while, baffled. Then the girl glanced at her watch and passed a hand wearily across her forehead.

'Half after one!'

'Want to sleep?' Larry asked her quietly.

'I did — but not any more. I've only one anxiety now and that is to get out of this ghastly place with a whole skin. Our only hope seems to be that power plant, wherever it is. Let's look around — '

'We leave him?' Larry gestured to Drew.

'Why not?' the girl tossed over her shoulder, heading for the Library doorway. 'If the current is still on, and I suppose it is, we can't touch him without getting it.'

Larry followed her out of the room wondering why he had not himself thought of such an elementary fact. They were both in the hall when a vast pounding din on the front door whirled them round with thumping hearts.

'Poole!' Larry gasped abruptly. 'By

heaven, it must be he!' He dived for the obdurate front door and beat fiercely upon it.

'Hello there! *Hello! Can you hear me?*' he bawled.

'That you, Larry?' came Poole's familiar voice, so far away he sounded as if he were at the end of a long tunnel. 'What the devil's going on in there? Open the door!'

'We can't; it's sealed electrically, and all the windows have steel shutters on the inside. Even the walls and floors are steel lined. The place is a death trap. Drew, de Brock, Valant and Darnhome have all died. Only one man can get us out of here and that's Quinton. Haven't you seen him?'

'Seen him?' repeated the distant voice. 'Why should I?'

'He's left a talkie film here and says he is giving himself up to Scotland Yard.'

'The devil he is! We must have missed him, then. I started out for Tifley the moment you phoned because I didn't like the sound of things. It's taken us all this time to find you. And you say you can't get out? There must be *some* way!'

Shouting until his throat was dry Larry made the position clear.

'All right, I see how things are,' Poole responded. 'I'll have Bryant hop to the nearest telephone in the car and get in touch with the Yard. If Quinton's there he can be flown here straight away. In the meantime we'll look around and see if we can dig into this place from outside, even if only to get food in to you in case Quinton hasn't turned up at the Yard. How about blasting? Could we risk that?'

'It might work. I don't care what you do.'

'Right. And by the way, the Commissioner let me know who Joyce Sutton really is. Told me when I reported I was coming up to Tifley. She's still okay, you say?'

'Right here beside me. All right, chief, you see what you can do and we'll scout around and try and locate that power plant. If we can find it and disable it our worries will be over — I hope!'

'Okay!'

'Come on,' Larry said, turning and

catching the girl's arm. 'We'll comb this place inside out. Kitchen first, where the sound seems to be loudest.'

They hurried through the length of the hall and into that small, square room with its steel-plated wall disguised to look like tiling. Regardless now of possible booby traps — for they both had the inner conviction that very few other things would be taped now that Drew had met his fate in ordered sequence — they examined the sink, the refrigerator, the cupboards, the drawers. They lay on the floor and listened — all to no purpose.

'No use,' Larry sighed. 'No secret switches or anything.'

'Suppose,' the girl said, scrambling up again, 'we don't bother trying but just wait for either Quinton to turn up or the Inspector to dig his way in?'

'Because both might fail! Don't you see that, Virgie? We've got to help ourselves. I think Quinton would be clever enough to make the foundations of this house impenetrable, and if he didn't go to Scotland Yard after all, or perhaps even met with an accident, we'll simply starve to death! No, we've got to try everything. Let's go over the lounge and library.' They took the library first, and as in the case of the kitchen explored it thoroughly, with exactly similar results. It was the same in the lounge, in the dining room, in the bedrooms — everywhere.

They even examined each one of the stairs minutely, until at last, weary with futility, they returned slowly to the hall and looked at each other. Then Larry went across to the front door and shouted. There was no response.

'Either gone for tools, explosives or something,' he said, returning to the girl as she stifled a yawn.

'Quarter to three,' she said, glancing at her watch. 'This is about the longest night I ever spent.'

She sat down heavily on the second stair and leaned her head back against the balustrade uprights. Larry, squatted beside her and pulled out his cigarette case, proffered it.

'Thanks,' she muttered, taking one, and he lit it for her. 'Might help to keep me awake, anyhow.'

For a space they sat watching the smoke curling up in the dim light.

'One thing I'm wondering,' Larry said at length. 'I wonder what keeps the power plant going? There's no electricity laid on this remote spot, surely? No main cable, I mean.'

'I've thought of that,' the girl answered. 'Only answer I can see is a turbo-generator, set up somewhere near a strong brook or stream. There are plenty of those in the hills near here. That would explain it, and power transmitted from that spot.'

'Mmm,' Larry admitted. 'Looks like you may be right — and Quinton seems to have thought of everything . . . ' For a while he mused; then, 'I wonder if there *is* a way out of this confounded place? And I'll tell you where: through the partition occupied at present by the glass screen on which Quinton's face appeared.'

'Why should that lead to a way out?'

'I don't say that it will — but it might be worth a try. As a final ironic gesture Quinton might have left a loophole — and if there is one that is the only place.'

'Maybe,' the girl admitted. 'But how do we know the steel door itself isn't electrified?'

'We don't. We could find out by throwing my cigarette case at it. If there's a spark we can be pretty sure what's wrong.' Larry got to his feet, tossed down his cigarette on the plated hall floor and stamped on it. 'Come on! No reason why we should be beaten.'

Virginia got up and followed him across the hall into the library, throwing down and stamping on her cigarette as she went. They stood looking at the sprawled body of Drew for a while, then Larry took out his cigarette case and tossed it down so that opposite edges struck door and metal floor simultaneously. There was no trace of a spark. On the copper vase it was different. There was a brief distinct flash.

'That's still alive and the door's free,' he said. 'All right, I'm going to risk it.'

The girl watched him tensely as he reached out and touched the cold steel of the door. Then he relaxed, his brow shiny.

'Okay. Quite dead. Hand me that chair, please.'

She pulled across a hard-backed chair and he climbed on to it and banged the point of his elbow into the glass partition. It went flying inwards in a tinkle of falling shards. Intently, standing tiptoe, he peered into the gap beyond.

'Anything visible?' the girl asked anxiously, standing below him.

'No. At least not much. I can see something about the size of a large coin gleaming, and unless I miss my guess it's the lens of the projector that showed that Quinton picture. But I can hear something!' Larry added, his voice sharpening.

'What?'

'Yes!' he confirmed excitedly. 'It's the power plant! It's quite distinct from behind this door. Damn! If only there were a light beyond here.'

'What about your lighter?'

'Running out of fuel; no more than a glimmer. I'm going to chance it anyway. Here I go.'

He elbowed away the remaining glass carefully and then gripped the edge of the frame and began to haul himself up. Wriggling and shoving, his legs waving wildly, he eased himself through the narrow square and felt out blindly into the dark beyond. He was in a position where he could not see where he was going and could not turn round either — so he shoved himself forward and dropped head first into the abyss. He landed on something hard and metallic, his shoulder jarring.

'Are you all right?' the girl called anxiously, and he got up to see her head framed in the opening as she stood on the chair.

'Near as can be, but I'd sooner be tucked comfortably in bed. Wait a moment: I'll see if there's a way of opening this door.'

He struck up his waning lighter and held the glimmer of flame close to the steel. To his satisfaction he found a steel bolt with a curiously-fashioned plunger at the end fixed on the bottom of the door. He pulled the plunger gingerly at first, then with abrupt effort. The bolt shot back and the door swung inwards towards the library.

Virginia stood beyond, obviously surprised.

'All right so far,' Larry breathed. 'Come on.'

The girl moved forward cautiously and joined him in the gloom. Then she rubbed the sole of her shoe investigatingly along the floor.

'What are we standing on? It's ridged.'

'I noticed that. Feels like a grid or something. Anyway, do you hear that?'

They stood listening, holding on to each other, the light from the library barely reaching to where they were. There was no doubt now of the steady drone of power comparatively near to them, yet as it had been in the kitchen so it was now — somewhere beneath them.

'I should think we might — '

Whatever Larry was going to say was snapped off short as there was a sudden grinding crash. Behind them the oblong opening that gave on to the lighted library blotted out with a clash of metal striking metal as the door shut itself.

Simultaneously a steel slide banged adamantly into place exactly over the square where the glass screen had been. Evidently it had been drawn back flat against the wall and now a powerful spring action had released it.

Neither Virginia nor Larry spoke for a moment but they could hear each other breathing harshly in the darkness . . .

13

'My God!' Larry gasped at length. 'What damned fools we were! We should have wedged that door. It only stayed open for about a minute. Hang on to me.'

They groped their way back towards it, against the steel wall of the narrow passage. After some fumbling Larry brought out his lighter, but the flint sparked uselessly on a dry wick. Muttering to himself he pushed the lighter back in his pocket and felt around for the plunger device on the door. He found it at length and pulled hard, but nothing happened. Some inexorable mechanism had snapped into position and the door was solidly, immovably shut.

'No — use?' the girl whispered, and he could feel her hand on his arm trembling.

'No,' he said, in a voice that sounded ghostly.

Darkness. Utter darkness. And that maddening hum somewhere below.

'Larry,' the girl breathed. ' I'm scared! And I'm not ashamed to admit it.'

'That's about the most womanly thing you've said so far,' he murmured, 'and I love you for it — ' He patted her arm and stirred slowly. 'Well, there's no way back, so maybe we'd better try going forward. Are you game?'

'No alternative.'

They clung to each other and felt their way along the cold, steely, humming abyss. A foot — two feet — a yard. Then all of a sudden, so bewildering that it was blinding, there was a brilliant flood, of light below them from two electric globes. For a moment or two they clapped their hands over their eyes and accustomed themselves.

'Great heavens!' Virginia exclaimed finally. 'Where *are* we?'

Larry did not answer. They gazed about them in wonderment. They were in a big, completely square room — or at any rate some kind of chamber. It was large, about fifteen feet square, with walls of gleaming metal. The ceiling, also of metal, the rivets on the plates clearly visible, was about twelve feet above them.

These facts they noticed in a moment or so, then they came to speculating about the floor. It was a complete grating, a metal fishnet pattern, which with the lights set well below it cast a filigree shadow on the metal walls of the chamber.

'Look!' Virginia pointed down beneath their feet.

They silently contemplated a softly humming electric power plant. There was a dynamo, glowing radio-tubes, potentiometers, resistances — a marvelously constructed though small unit with a multitude of wires leading from it.

'We've found it!' Larry said, soberly. 'The power plant from where all the dirty work is done, and probably powered by a turbo-generator somewhere, as you yourself theorized. See that cable there? It follows all the way up to the projector.'

They turned and looked behind them, able now to see the projector that had carried the sound-print of Quinton. It was perched on a high shelf above the passage way.

'And all the other gadgets work in the same fashion,' the girl said. 'Like mechanical dolls in a store.' She knelt down on the grating and peered below. 'But we can't get through this grating and stop the plant. Any ideas?'

Larry settled beside her, both their faces criss-crossed with the metallic fishnet shadow.

'None,' he muttered. 'Except explore and see if part of this grating comes away somewhere. I can't somehow get the idea of this,' he went on pensively, standing up again and helping the girl to rise beside him. 'Why did Quinton make it possible to get in here, to see the whole works nakedly exposed, arrange the door so that it shut, and then just leave it at that? Of course we could die in here from sheer starvation and exhaustion, but — That doesn't sound like the right answer. You'd think a man like Quinton would plan something more elaborate. Anyway, let's see what we have.'

They turned and investigated the walls and the grating-floor, but minutely though they explored there was no sign of a crack or means of getting down into that softly humming power plant.

Then the girl gripped Larry's arm tightly.

'Larry!' Her voice was tense, brittle with dread. He looked at her in surprise to find her staring above.

'What?'

'I — I don't know. Maybe it's because I'm not wearing my glasses, but — I thought I saw the ceiling *move*!'

'The ceiling?' Larry jerked his head back and they both watched the ceiling's shadowed metal smoothness. For a moment or two nothing happened — then the square crept down perhaps an inch and became still again.

'It *did* move!' Virginia shouted hoarsely.

'Yes.' Larry found his throat dry as dust. He just couldn't take his eyes from the gray square. There was no longer any doubt. The ceiling was lowering, inexorably, inch by inch.

'Larry, we've *got* to get out!' the girl cried, shaking him. 'Don't you understand? Don't you *see*? We'll be crushed — '

He tore his eyes away from the ceiling

and stared at her.

'But where do we go? How?'

The girl dashed across the grating and to the steel slide in the narrow passage just beyond the room proper. She battered at the metal with her naked fists, tore at the ground level bolt, until the sheer futility of it made her stop. With a ghostly face she came back to where Larry was looking into the power plant and then up at the ceiling.

'At least I get the idea,' he said bitterly. 'Quinton made this chamber end passage his last trump card. In case any of the men got through the gauntlet of his other devices he left a way to get into here — through the glass screen over the steel door — which way we took. He knew that on the inside the door would shut. Then perhaps we passed an invisible photo-electric beam across this chamber somewhere which started the ceiling mechanism and — '

'Shut up!' the girl screamed at him. 'What do the mechanics matter? This room is a hydraulic press and the ceiling and floor are plates! Oh, my God, what do we *do*?'

But the mechanics of the horror still seemed to fascinate Larry more than the prospect of imminent death.

'The ingenuity of it,' he breathed. 'If lights had been fixed in the ceiling we could perhaps have short-circuited the socket and stopped the machine — but Quinton has guarded against that by putting the lights under our feet out of reach! Damnation! If only I'd thought to fuse one of the lights in the house! It might have stopped the whole caboosh. Mightn't though. A separate circuit perhaps. Begins to look to me as though Quinton is our only hope of ever getting out of this lot alive.'

'Things like that don't happen,' the girl said dully. 'There's nothing we can do.'

Larry put an arm about her trembling shoulders. The ceiling seemed to have increased its rate of descent now. With dull rumbles it was jerking down relentlessly. There was a thunderous crash as the projector on its shelf was smashed down and fell to the floor of the passage.

It was only just above their heads as Larry and Virginia clung to each other.

Inevitably they were forced to their knees. There seemed to be no words they could utter. Their tongues were paralyzed; their lips burning. Somehow Larry struggled to speak.

'We've — we've got to lie down.'

The girl stretched herself beside him and stared for a moment at the gray square dropping. Then she screamed frantically.

'Larry, I can't *bear* it! I can't lie here and watch it coming down on me — '

'Turn over on your face!' he snapped, sweating.

'I — I can't — ' Virginia was shuddering. 'I — I can't do it! This thing — coming down — not seeing it — waiting for it to crack my spine . . . *Oh, my God!*'

She fought desperately to keep control of her senses, wriggled into a sideways position. Even Larry found the vision of watching that square too much for him. He turned heavily on to his right side and wondered vaguely what it was that crunched and ground beneath him. He put an arm about the girl's quivering body. Unbreathable oppression was upon them.

Larry flattened himself to the limit and felt wetness clinging round the seat of his pants. He just couldn't understand why. The first cold steel touch settled on his cheek as he raised his head slightly. Virginia made a slight motion, and fainted —

But ... the ceiling had stopped lowering! Larry lay rigid, trying to fathom it out. It seemed too that the humming from the power plant had stopped. The ceiling metal rubbed his head as he twisted and looked below. The two lights still burned, but they were wavering as though the power, perhaps stored up as potential, was giving out.

Only by slow degrees did Larry realize what had happened. The whisky flask he had taken from Darnhome and thrust in his pocket had smashed and dropped its three-quarters-full contents into the heart of the unit below, shorting it.

'God!' Larry uttered the word through cracked lips. 'I'll — I'll never blame a guy for drinking ever again!'

The lights below went out suddenly and the darkness was beyond imagining. Larry began to shift and wriggle, scared lest he might start the nearly closed trap working again. He began a slow, worming movement, hands out-thrust, and kept going until he felt the steel of the door at the end of the narrow passage. He fumbled and struggled until he found the bolt.

To his infinite relief it slid aside easily and a shove sent the door swinging inwards into the black library. Shaking so much he could hardly stand he felt around for a chair and jammed it against the slide, then he crawled back again down the narrow space between the plates until he found Virginia's feet. By hard pulling and effort he dragged her free of the death trap, hauled her up into his arms and then scrambled through the darkness until he found an armchair. Gently he settled her down.

'Virgie! Virgie!' He rubbed her wrists and at last felt her begin to stir. 'Virgie, we're safe! We're out!'

'Are we — are we dead?' Her voice

floated out of the abyss. 'Larry! I can't see!'

'Lights have failed . . . ' Words tumbled over themselves as Larry explained; then he felt her hands quivering in desperate relief.

'I'd forgotten all about that flask,' he hurried on. 'In fact I — '

He broke off, startled. There were sounds in the house for the first time, the tramp of heavy feet. Suddenly torches became dazzlingly visible in the room.

'So here you are!' Inspector Poole exclaimed.

'Chief!' Larry cried hoarsely. 'Thank God for that — How'd you get in? Has Quinton arrived?'

'No. I was standing on guard by the front door, leaning on it as a matter of fact, and it suddenly opened and I dropped inside! What happened?'

'Must have been when the power unit failed,' Larry muttered. 'We were nearly crushed to death — I'll tell you later. I — '

'There are three cars in the garage,' Poole said grimly, 'and two men shot dead. I suppose there's a reason for that?'

'Every reason. The servant must have done it — But what about Quinton? Where is he?'

Poole's voice sobered. 'We rang the Yard. It seems he turned up after we'd gone. He wrote a full confession, gave Scotland Yard power of attorney to do as they wish in handling his bomb, and then . . . he shot himself. In my office!'

Larry and Virginia said nothing. They both straightened up slowly from the chairs opposite each other.

'You two look about all in,' Poole said. 'Sergeant, give them a hand.'

They were helped out of the room and through the hall to the front door.

'Never again a night like this,' Larry whispered in the girl's ear.

'Never again,' she agreed quietly. 'The nights we'll have will be very, very different . . . '

They had come into the sweet moorland air. Far away to the east the dawn was breaking . . .